MAKING IT BETTER

LYSS EM

ACKNOWLEDGMENTS

Thank you to Tanya Chris for helping me out significantly with this book's description.

And a very special thank-you to the following Patreon patrons:

- Vivien Del
- Angelica Santana
- Camila

Your support means the world to me.

To C–
Thnks fr th mmrs.

CHAPTER 1

LUCAN and the man making him shudder with pleasure were just friends. The undulating music permeating the BDSM dungeon fell into the background as Dom rolled a Wartenburg wheel up the backs of Lucan's legs, across his shoulder blades, and down his spine. The sensation disappeared for a moment, and then the spikes were pricking the bottom of Lucan's foot. On the massage table, Lucan groaned into his arms folded beneath his head and tried to keep his thrashing to a minimum.

Lucan didn't much like his feet played with, but Dom liked it. Dom especially liked when Lucan couldn't control what his body did, and Lucan was getting there. He was right on the edge of subspace. Just a moment more...

Dom squeezed Lucan's shoulder and whispered into his ear, "Okay?"

"Green," said Lucan, which meant "Keep going."

A rustling told him that Dom was rummaging in his toy bag. Then, the rustling stopped. Dom's feet brushed the cement floor of the dungeon, and Lucan's stomach did a flip. The next implement would either be a light impact toy, which was fine but not Lucan's favorite, or a—

Cool metal chilled Lucan's shoulder, and a sound he barely

recognized crawled out of his throat. He'd been expecting something ticklish and soft like a feather—not a knife. Knives weren't on his limits list, though, and per his and Dom's agreement that anything else was fair game, knives were allowed.

Dom trailed the edge of the dulled blade down Lucan's back to just above the band of his blue boxer briefs. Lucan didn't usually get hard during their play, but he couldn't help it this time. The arousal made his whole groin feel heavy. Nothing existed but the blade and its path along his sensitive skin, taking him simultaneously into the atmosphere and deeper into the massage table. He sunk into the warm leather yet flew high as the blade fondled his nerves.

Dom's breath fanned his ear. "You're perfect right now."

Green, Lucan thought but couldn't say. *More, please.*

Dom's warmth disappeared and the blade, cold again—a new blade—touched the inside of Lucan's thigh. He jerked, and his whole body throbbed.

No! I can't get this high, he thought. *Not with Dom. This is supposed to be casual.* But at the same time, the most primal part of him whispered, *More, more, more. Let Dom take care of me. I could be* his.

The urge to be owned was beyond inappropriate here. So Lucan had to put a stop to this pleasure, no matter how good it felt. "Red," he croaked.

All metallic sensations ceased. Dom's footsteps came quick—*brush-brush-brush-brush*—then Dom was looking into Lucan's eyes with his own eyes wide with worry. They were dark, kind. Dom's warm brown skin had a panicked—or aroused?—sheen to it.

"It's over. Are you okay?" he asked.

The music was too loud. Some people were talking and laughing at the edge of the playroom—fucking rude, but that was the kind of behavior one could expect at a TNG (The Next Generation) party, where attendees were from age eighteen to thirty-five but mostly early twenties. Lucan himself was twenty-seven, but he knew how to not be a dick.

Lucan pushed himself up and slid off the massage table, landing on shaky feet. Dom was at his side, trying to support him, but Lucan nudged him and his invitingly hot skin away. "Just get me some water, please."

As soon as Dom had disappeared toward the kitchen, Lucan headed to the bathroom. Dom would understand that he needed a moment.

After slamming the door shut and turning its lock, Lucan shoved down his briefs and gripped his still-stiff cock. He needed to get rid of the hard-on so it wouldn't become a *thing* with Dom. He'd probably noticed already, but he wouldn't mention it if it was gone by the time they started aftercare, and with how red and swollen he was, there was no way this would go down in the next couple of minutes on its own.

Standing over the toilet, Lucan stroked himself roughly, only a little precum there to temper the friction. He pictured what he always pictured when he jacked off—Court, his ex. Not the last guy he'd dated, but the last to *own* him, to take him to that place much more intense than the endorphin rush and relaxation that came with casual play— the place Dom could have taken him just now if he'd let him.

Lucan knew it was pathetic to still be thinking about Court years later, but there was something about being pathetic that Lucan kind of liked—so long as he was hidden away like this where Dom and everybody else he respected couldn't see.

He pictured the time Court had made him bleed. He'd taken a kitchen knife to Lucan's stomach, swiped the blood with his thumb, and rubbed it on Lucan's mouth. Lucan remembered with painstaking clarity the cool, textured surface of the refrigerator door against his cheek as Court fucked him. Court's hand had come up into Lucan's line of vision, slamming against the door and smearing blood against it, and Lucan had soared like he'd done with Dom but to a much greater degree—with his eyes open, his ass full, and his heart bleeding as much as his stomach. He had come so hard, and Court had whispered into his ear, "You're mine, Luc. Don't ever forget that." It had been Heaven hearing those words.

Lucan bit his tongue to keep from shouting as he finished, his cum hitting the water in the toilet bowl. He flushed it and sighed against a pain in his stomach. It was psychosomatic, something that often hit him on the comedown. He and Dom usually curled up somewhere with Lucan's head in Dom's lap, but he wasn't sure he wanted that tonight. He felt naked, like someone had taken his skin off.

A knock sounded on the bathroom door. "Lucan? You in there?"

Lucan pulled up his underwear, then opened the door.

Dom handed him a chilled bottle of water. "Let me look at your back."

"It's fine." Lucan pushed past him, heading for the sitting room the owners of the house had set up as a social space.

Dom gripped Lucan's wrist, and Lucan yanked it away violently, glaring at Dom. Dom wasn't usually forceful with Lucan, and Lucan didn't want that kind of treatment from him.

But Dom's gaze grew soft and hurt, and guilt washed over Lucan.

"Are you going to deny me aftercare?" Dom asked.

It was something they'd talked about before. Everybody acted like bottoms were the only ones who needed aftercare, but one of Dom's crusades was that Tops needed it, too.

Lucan agreed. "No," he said. "I'm sorry. What do you need?"

Dom straightened. Lucan had never said it out loud, but Dom's short and skinny dreadlocks, hanging in his eyes and a little past his ears, made him look adorable even when he was in Serious Top Mode.

"Go find a place to sit." Dom pointed in the direction of the sitting room. "I'll be there in a minute."

Lucan gripped his bottled water hard enough for the plastic to crunch. He could tell Dom that he didn't want to be touched anymore tonight, that he just wanted to be alone and that his back was fine. But Lucan knew all too well how cruel it was to deny someone what they needed after a scene. In a couple days, if Lucan experienced any type of bottom drop, Dom would be there to talk things through, cuddle, whatever—no questions asked. Lucan owed him the same level of courtesy.

He found an empty sofa and sat down.

* * *

Court couldn't decide if he looked ridiculous or fine as hell wearing the leather harness. He was pretty sure he had it on correctly, at least. The thick black straps hugged him across the chest and over the shoulders and connected to an O-ring at his back.

The tightness made him feel a little funny in the stomach. He'd rather have a person holding him than leather, but that was the whole point of tonight. It was time to get out there and find someone kinky enough to please him. Court needed a boyfriend—a steady one—and the party was a good first step. He'd managed to get permission to attend the invite-only venue after going to a few BDSM munches.

This was his very first party in the scene. He wanted to look good. But if he stood here staring at himself any longer, he was going to be unfashionably late. He shrugged on his suit jacket—oh yeah, now he looked perfect—and grabbed his keys before heading out.

Half an hour later, he'd finally managed to locate the house with his maps app. The two-story Victorian stood dark and apparently lifeless, but there were several cars parked outside and all the way to the corner. Court had to parallel park a street over.

The short walk didn't do anything for his nerves. By the time he was standing on the stoop, his heart was pounding, and he was regretting not wearing a shirt under the harness. In his mirror at home, it had seemed fine, but with the summer breeze blowing across his nipples, he felt much too exposed. But he hadn't brought any other clothes, and he wasn't going to bail. Who knew when he'd get another invitation like this?

With a deep breath, he knocked on the door. When no one answered, he knocked again...and again.

The door opened to reveal a heavyset young woman with a collar at her throat. "You don't have to knock. You can just come in."

Court laughed nervously. "Oh. Sorry."

The woman led him into the foyer and to a plastic table with some papers on it. Behind her, a black curtain served as a makeshift wall.

"You're new?" she asked.

"Isn't it obvious?"

She gave Court an indulgent smile. "Please read over the house rules and sign in. Then you can join the party."

Tension settled over Court's shoulders as he stood there in silence trying to read the rules. He mostly skimmed. No touching anyone without consent, no playing drunk (seemed like a good idea), no watersports except in designated areas, etc. He checked off a box saying he'd read the rules, then signed his name. Next, he signed in on a sheet holding about fifty usernames from FetNet, the social media site everybody in the scene used. Court added his own username, MisterK289.

"Tribute's fifteen dollars," said the young woman. "And I'll need to see your ID."

Right—"tribute" as in a required donation. Court was still getting used to the wording the community had to use in case of any legal trouble. Even though it made him uncomfortable to show his ID, he figured it was so the owners of the house could be sure he was eighteen. He was twenty-nine, but his smooth face and athletic appearance sometimes had people pegging him as younger.

"You're all set." The woman gestured behind her. "The curtains open in the middle."

Court approached the black fabric warily and pawed at it until he found the opening. From the other side, he could hear the woman laughing at him. *Geez.* Could he be any more awkward?

Behind the curtain was the rest of the foyer, one closed door marked "CHANGING ROOM," and an open closet with a few garments, including a trench coat, hanging inside. A second curtain blocked off whatever part of the house was to the left, and up ahead, laughter and chatter drifted from an interior archway.

Court braced himself. Would he see anyone he recognized from the events he'd already attended? He knew the owners of the house were an older Domme and boy couple who rented out the place for parties like these. He'd met the Domme at a munch, but would she even be here?

He swallowed and headed toward the party.

The archway led to a kitchen full of people. Instantly

claustrophobic, Court hung near the wall, running his gaze over the guests standing around, most of them holding drinks. Court had never seen this many pairs of fishnets in one place, nor leather, and he didn't feel as naked as he had outside. But then people started to notice him. A blonde girl in stilettos eyed him predatorily, and a muscly guy looked him up and down, bringing heat to Court's skin. Neither were his type, though. He edged past the people and through another archway.

The next room was darker and noticeably hotter. A bass beat made the air vibrate, and rhythmic slapping noises came from more than one direction. As Court's eyes adjusted, he made out bodies. Someone gripped a big wooden X while a man hit their back and ass with something bendy. A woman lay over another kind of contraption while another woman spanked her. Some people gathered on one side of the room and chatted quietly—spectators?

Then a moan found Court's ears. And it was utterly familiar, and it wound through his whole body like a thorned bunch of vines until his heart constricted, and the back of his neck pricked.

Lucan.

It couldn't be. Then again, it was possible Court's ex had returned to Pittsburgh. Not that Court would know; Lucan had blocked him on all social media. But he'd heard from a mutual friend that Lucan had moved to Detroit. If he was back, it made perfect sense that he was *here* —at a party for his and Court's age group where people did all the kinky things they'd used to do together. Court could remember slapping Lucan's ass purple like it was yesterday.

Fuck, fuck, fuck. Should Court leave? Well, no. That'd be pathetic. It had been years since they'd broken up—six, to be exact.

But he needed to play it cool. Eventually, he'd have to leave this dark-ass room, and if he stayed at this party long enough, Lucan would see him. He'd *have* to see Court in this sexy outfit, looking way more ripped than he'd been back then.

So, really, it was perfect. Court could say hi, say he was new to the scene and relieved to see a familiar face, which would be true, technically, and maybe Lucan wouldn't look at him like he'd last looked at him—like all the times Court had hurt him hadn't been consensual or something. Like Court had done something really wrong. Lucan had never told him what that might be. He had just said it was over, and then he'd gone silent, and the next time Court had seen him had been in passing on Pitt's campus.

Memories of Lucan Burke had been hiding in the back of Court's mind for the past few years, but they were back now, clear and cutting.

Court found a bit of wall to lean against and closed his eyes. As he'd learned to do whenever he got overloaded with adrenaline, he focused on his breathing, but also on the bass beat and the slaps.

CHAPTER 2

LUCAN SAT SIDEWAYS on the big leather couch while Dom ran a rubbing alcohol swab up and down his back, sending the flesh smarting but only slightly. Dom had gone very easy on Lucan tonight as he pretty much always did. He was a gentle Top, and though Lucan enjoyed pain, he and Dom had agreed never to cross that line with each other. Pain made Lucan feel needy and submissive—out of control—and Dom didn't enjoy making his bottoms cry or bleed.

Lucan had quickly learned about Dom when they'd met about three years back. As Lucan got comfortable with his head in Dom's lap, the memory of their first encounter at a BDSM munch floated behind his eyes. "I probably won't stay in the scene much longer," Dom had said. "I want something vanilla in the end." But the lifestyle had a way of taking up all of someone's time, and the connections with fellow fetishists sunk into one like flesh hooks. As testament to that fact, Lucan and Dom lived with two other people in the scene, and pretty soon, they were planning to make their clique an official House. They just needed a cool name.

Lucan tried to think of something. Maybe they should highlight Dom's favorite kink since he was the one who'd been in the scene the longest (though not long compared to the true kink veterans). House of Sensation? Sensational House? House of...

"So." Dom squeezed Lucan's shoulder gently. "Are knives off the table now?"

Talking about a scene afterward was important, but Lucan often found it tedious with Dom since they stayed within a clearly planned box that involved very little risk to their bodies, minds, and hearts. Tonight, things were different but no more fun. Since the scene hadn't gone as hoped, awkwardness hung like an odor between them. It wasn't often Lucan called red during a scene, or even yellow.

"Yeah," Lucan said. "At least for a while. Triggered a memory for me." It was a half-truth, but it was less anxiety-inducing than telling Dom they'd almost crossed a mental line. Later, when he was feeling less shaken, he'd bring it up. Maybe.

"Oh?" Dom asked.

Now Dom would want to talk about the memory, but Lucan had already orgasmed it out of his system. It didn't matter. None of that shit with Court mattered; it was just like watching old porn clips at this point—or so Lucan told himself.

"Let's not go any deeper with this," said Lucan.

He didn't need to look at Dom to know he was rolling his eyes.

"Whatever makes you happy," Dom said.

"You petting me makes me happy." Lucan looked up at Dom with his best submissive eyes, and Dom smirked and resumed stroking Lucan's hair. The familiar physical intimacy got rid of the awkwardness, replacing it with warmth and safety. Dom was a constant and consistent presence in Lucan's life, always taking care of him in the right ways even if outwardly, Lucan resisted.

Lucan closed his eyes and drank in the easy attention. Untold minutes passed.

Then a voice that didn't belong to Dom shattered Lucan's contentment. "Hey." That one syllable reeked of familiarity, and it threatened to tug Lucan down into hot, dangerous memories.

He snapped his eyes open. There, standing in front of him, was the star of Lucan's masturbation fantasies: Court. *Court* was here.

Lucan blinked several times before he accepted that he wasn't hallucinating. Then, his panicked heartbeat thundering through every limb, he scrambled from Dom's lap, sending Dom grunting as their bones and muscles bumped into each other.

"It's so nice to see a familiar face," said Court. He flashed his celebrity smile—straight teeth, full lips, squinty eyes. It had made Lucan melt when he'd met him a lifetime ago; now, it made him want to throw up.

He found his footing and was suddenly all too aware of his half-naked state. He was only wearing his boxer briefs, and it usually didn't matter because a lot of people were half-naked at play parties.

Tonight, that included Court. Lucan took him in from the tips of his shoes to the shiny belt holding up his trousers, then to the skin, the leather. The harness peeked out from between the lapels of his suit jacket, and Lucan had never seen a more aesthetically appealing outfit in his life. And his face... How was he so happy to see Lucan despite everything that had happened between them?

Was Court being here Lucan's fault? Had he conjured him up with the moments he'd been reliving over and over for far too long?

"Lucan, is everything okay?" Dom, standing now, touched Lucan's shoulder.

Lucan shook away from the touch. "Yeah. It's all good." He tore his gaze from Court.

Fuck! Court was here!

"We were just leaving, right, Dom? Heading out?" Lucan asked.

Concern put a crease between Dom's brows. "Yeah, sure, if you're ready."

"I'm ready. I'm *so* fucking ready." Lucan had been back in his hometown for a few months, and he'd known that it was only a matter of time before he'd run into Court—maybe at the restaurant where he worked and often saw people from high school or his time at Pitt—but he couldn't do this right now. Court's stomach-churning, dick-hardening presence did not belong in Lucan's safe space, in his community. Lucan's past did not belong *here*.

As Lucan turned to follow Dom to the front closet where their clothes were, hot fingers curled above the crook of his arm.

Terror and fury gripped Lucan. He fixed his incredulous gaze on

Court's determined one. "Touching people without consent can get you thrown out of here."

Court's grip didn't budge, and no matter how much he didn't want it to, Lucan's world dissolved into that one sensation of skin on skin and his muscle vised in Court's hand. Court was no longer smiling; his all-American features had hardened with a beautiful combination of arrogance and offense. This interaction tasted of how they'd used to be, with Court touching Lucan whenever he wanted and however he wanted, no matter Lucan's reaction to it. Their relationship hadn't been healthy, but Court taking control by force or otherwise had never failed to make Lucan's whole body hot and alive.

Now, Lucan's spent and thoroughly confused cock gave an interested twitch, but bodily reactions were one thing, and Court's violation was another. This wasn't okay. Where was Dom? He must have already left the house. Did he think Lucan was behind him?

"Let me go," Lucan said.

"Was that your boyfriend?" asked Court.

"Yes," Lucan lied.

Court released Lucan's arm, leaving an ache behind, but it disappeared after a couple of throbs. Lucan found it hard to move now that he was free. Maybe because Court didn't move, either, and there was a dark flush at Court's throat, and his exposed nipples were hard, and that fucking harness looked so good on him.

Lucan touched his arm where Court had touched it. Nobody had grabbed him like that—hard enough to hurt—in such a long time.

"Is there a problem here?" The deep voice of Griffin, tonight's Dungeon Master, pulled Lucan from his trance.

Lucan looked at Court, whose eyes were wide like he'd never experienced a consequence in his life, and then at Griffin, who was giving his best intimidating stare. He was beefy and bearded with strong arms and a hefty gut, and Lucan had watched him put a guy in a chokehold once for not obeying a bottom's safeword.

Lucan could get Court thrown out, if he wanted. He could get him blacklisted from the venue if he pushed. But something stopped him.

"Everything's fine," he said. "Thanks for looking out, Griff."

"You're welcome." Griffin gave Court a last hard glare before stepping aside, revealing Dom, who was a little taller than Griffin but much thinner.

Dom gave Court a glare as well. "Come on, Lucan." He settled a protective hand at Lucan's lower back and nudged him toward the front of the house. Not bothering with the changing room, they got dressed in the foyer, and Lucan looked at himself in the mirrored side of the closet door. He looked wrecked, with bags under his eyes and his dyed-blond hair mussed from Dom playing with it.

"Who was that?" Dom asked.

My Dominant, Lucan's body whispered. But that voice belonged to the innocent kid Court had ensnared back then. The Lucan of today was not a slave to his needy, pain-loving, submissive side.

"Remember the ex I told you about who regularly failed to give me aftercare?" Lucan asked.

"Shit."

"Exactly." The pain in Lucan's stomach was back, spreading like some internal herpes breakout. "I hate him." Lucan watched the fire build in his own eyes.

Dom tapped him on the shoulder. "Stop staring at yourself, Narcissus."

Desperation scratched Lucan everywhere. "I can't deal with him, Dom."

"You don't have to." Dom wrapped an arm around Lucan and guided him toward the house's exit. "Let's go home. Everything's going to be okay. I promise."

* * *

Court couldn't stay at the party. He'd had easy expectations for the evening; he'd planned to have a chill time, maybe meet a few people. But now that he'd known Lucan had been here—now that he'd left—everything was worthless.

Court slipped out and back into his car to make the twenty-minute drive to his apartment. All the while, Lucan occupied his thoughts.

Court had fucked up tonight, per usual. He shouldn't have grabbed Lucan like that and pissed him off. But seeing Lucan had brought Court right back to all the times they'd spent together. There hadn't been anything stopping him from grabbing Lucan then, shoving him wherever he wanted, doing as he pleased to that hot little body. Though if Court was being honest, it didn't matter much what Lucan looked like. It was his attitude, his sharpness. It was how that sharpness faded to soft, supple edges whenever Court found another thing that flipped the kid. A knife against his flesh—that did it. And God, was there anything better than having someone's blood smeared on your fingers? A good long spanking session made Lucan soft, too, but not as quickly. Those had been for nights when they'd both needed to escape. Maybe Lucan had a huge test coming up, or Court had just gotten off the phone with his stupid dad.

They hadn't been so good together the rest of the time. Couldn't talk about feelings or the future without fighting. The last time they'd had sex, it had been because Lucan had driven Court into a fit of jealousy by flirting with Court's frat brother Ash. And it had been intentional, too. Court could be a possessive asshole sometimes, but he trusted Ash. They were still friends to this day. He would never have lost it if Lucan hadn't looked Ash dead in the eye with his come-fuck-me expression *multiple* times, licking and biting his lips and everything, and Court had snapped. He'd taken him to his room and thrown him into the wall. "Are you trying to get Ash and I to have a threesome with you or something? Because it's never going to happen. He's barely bi."

"Maybe I just want to fuck him on my own," Lucan had said.

Court had fucked him more roughly than ever that night. He'd left bruises on him, bloody scratches. They'd gone so deep into it that afterward, Lucan had fallen to his knees at Court's feet. Court had barely been able to stand, and he'd wobbled as Lucan wrapped his arms around his leg, kissed his knee, and said, "I love you." The first time—and the only time—either one of them had said those words. Of course, Court had been in love since he'd met him.

The street sign coming up on Court's right alerted him to the fact he'd missed a turn. *Damn it.* He had to go in a circle because of

Pittsburgh's excess of fucking one-ways but eventually got back on track.

Would Lucan still have the same phone number he'd had when they were in school? It was a long shot, but Court's was the same. When he and his sister had moved out of Mom's house, they'd set up a new cell account together and transferred their numbers no problem.

But even if Court could text Lucan, he shouldn't. Lucan had a boyfriend. A very tall, very cute boyfriend. Court and Lucan had never cuddled the way he'd seen *them* doing. Lucan didn't like that kind of shit, or at least, he'd never let on that he liked it. He'd always asked Court to be rough with him, or more like he'd pushed Court to be that way, and they'd only gotten close when they'd slept in the same bed. Had Lucan secretly wanted cuddles and never said?

Court wanted to ask. But Lucan's eyes tonight... He'd looked at Court like he'd crossed some unspeakable line by touching him, and Court probably had. He wouldn't have done that with anyone but Lucan, and he couldn't just assume that after—what, six years?—he could do to Lucan what he'd always done. They hadn't so much as run into each other at the grocery store since Court had dropped out.

God, this was insane! Half of Court's brain was right back in the past, trembling with pain and desire at every fucked-up thing that had happened between them. The other half was still here in the present, struggling to come to terms with the fact that he and Lucan had been in the same room tonight—that Court had *touched* him. It had been sickeningly wonderful to feel Lucan's flesh in his grip again, soft on the outside but hard with muscle, hot, tense.

He should text Lucan and apologize for tonight. That wouldn't be weird. Just...polite, totally normal. He had all kinds of contacts in his phone that his cell company's cloud service kept transferring to each new device. Lucan's was probably in there. Court couldn't remember deleting it.

As soon as Court had parallel parked in front of his and Cally's apartment building, he went searching through his contacts. And there it was, an entry marked "Luc" with a smiling devil emoji next to it.

Skin buzzing, Court started a new text to the number.

Hey, this is Court. Don't know if this is still your number, but on the off chance it is, I want to say I'm sorry for tonight. Didn't mean to scare you or your boyfriend.

There. He'd done all he could to make things right, at least for the moment. If Lucan didn't answer his text, he might be able to contact him online. Court had used a social networking site, FetNet, to find the munches he'd gone to, and the party had an event page as well, with profiles attached as Attending or—

Court's phone vibrated.

Oh please. You didn't scare me, Court. Never have

A nauseous sort of excitement had sweat breaking out at Court's hairline. Suddenly, he was very aware of where the leather of his harness touched him. Boyfriend or not, maybe Court would get to feel Lucan wrapped around him again...

Sorry for offending you then, he answered. *Does your boyfriend wanna kick my ass?*

Dom's more mature than that. We could have had you blacklisted from every kink event in town, but we decided not to. You're welcome

A thank-you seemed a bit too...acquiescent. *I owe you one,* Court replied.

Seconds ticked by, then minutes. The conversation was clearly over, but Court couldn't control his hands. *You still mess me up after all this time, Luc.* He stopped short of telling him how thrilling it had been to be close to him again, to feel him in his grip.

Not my problem, Lucan replied. *And I don't care. Now leave me alone*

Court groaned his frustration at the shuttered response and threw his phone moodily into the passenger's seat.

CHAPTER 3

"Guys, look at his profile. Court is such a fucking *noob*." Lucan sat in the living room of his and his roommates' four-bedroom house with his computer screen projected onto the white wall. The projection was 100 inches wide and perfect for movie viewing but also for scrolling through FetNet as a group.

"This your ex?" asked Roland, the only straight, cisgender member of the household. He had shoulder-length straight hair and a mustache.

"That's right," said Lucan.

"Looks like a douche." That was rich considering Roland's own appearance and general demeanor, but Lucan wasn't in the mood to rag on him.

"I don't know, I think he's cute," said Erin. She was Roland's girlfriend and Lucan and Dom's fourth roommate.

Cute was an understatement, but Lucan was not in the mood for discussing Court's good qualities. He wanted to tear him to shreds. "He's an asshole," said Lucan. "He could have left a bruise on me last night." But he hadn't.

Dom pointed at the top portion of Court's profile. "Only interested in kink 'in the bedroom.' We all know that's just code for 'I saw *Fifty Shades of Grey* and got a semi.'" Dom, Erin, and Roland all laughed.

Lucan would have, too, except he knew that wasn't Court. Maybe he didn't want a 24/7 Dom/sub relationship these days, but he wasn't just dabbling in kink.

"Show us his pictures," said Erin.

Lucan hesitated. He hadn't yet looked at them himself. But the little *Photos* link underneath Court's profile picture—a shot of him smiling in a ball cap and Polo—had (5) next to it. Knowing what kinds of stuff users of FetNet were into, there would likely be some sexy pictures. Maybe even a dick pic.

"Come on," said Erin. "Don't make me squint at them on my phone."

With the little handheld mouse he and his roommates used to operate the projector, Lucan obliged.

The first photo was pretty tame: Court in a pair of leather pants and a black T-shirt. But in the second one, he was shirtless in a pair of low-hanging sweats that showed off his cut lower abdominal muscles.

Erin clicked her tongue and said, "Damn."

"This dude's gay, right?" Roland asked. "He's not gonna steal my girl?"

Erin punched Roland playfully on the bicep.

"Yeah, he's gay." Lucan clicked to the next picture.

Oh, fuck. There it was—Court's hard, glistening cock. It was so like him to post a picture like this! Lucan would have voiced his distaste if he wasn't immediately transported to the first time Court had sent him such a picture. He'd been in his dorm room at the naïve age of nineteen, and he'd felt so dirty under the covers on the top bunk, feeling hot and bothered by the kind of thing he'd never understood before. He hadn't thought the straight-looking frat boy from the party would make good on his word to text, but that was how it had started. Texts, pictures, orders, threats.

I'm going to make you suck this until you gag, Court had texted along with the pic. *You like that, babe?*

Lucan sprang up from the couch and yanked the adapter out of his laptop, causing the projection to disappear.

"Woah," said Erin.

"Um... You okay, Luc?" asked Dom.

"No." A million tiny ants skittered over Lucan's whole scalp. "Sorry, guys. I just need to...go." It was what he said when he got depressed. But right now, it was more that he needed to go for long walk in an empty neighborhood or make a late-night trip to a 24-hour supermarket, but it was three in the afternoon on a Sunday, and people would be *out*.

"No problem, man," said Roland.

Lucan made a beeline for his room, laptop in hand.

As soon as Lucan had shut the door, he sat on the bed cross-legged and reopened his laptop. Quickly, he navigated away from the picture of Court's dick and scrolled to the bottom of his profile page where his kinks were listed. Most people on FetNet had an extensive list of fetishes, and Court had a few of his own. Lucan chewed on a nail as he looked them over.

shoving him against the wall (giving), grabbing my sub's wrist (giving), hand over mouth (giving), mind games, an intense emotional connection, when the sex is so good they cry (giving)

A shiver hit the back of Lucan's neck. For a weak moment, he closed his eyes and let his mind go into a fantasy that was half memory and half imagination. Riding Court, slow, savoring the pleasure, hands on Court's muscular shoulders, hot tears welling and spilling down his already sweaty cheeks.

Face burning even though no one could see his sordid thoughts, Lucan opened his eyes and read over Court's list of "curious about" fetishes.

pulling his hair then petting him gently (giving), sitting at my owner's feet (receiving), cuddling as aftercare

The last one sent Lucan laughing, the sound false to his own ears. Court was *not* a cuddler. He fell right to sleep after sex every single time. Maybe he'd be up for it after a kink scene with no sex involved, but if Court got the least bit horny during the scene, no dice. He was pushy about sex. Lucan had never had cause to complain about that, but they'd never set explicit limits, either. How would Court act if he wanted sex after his bottom had already said no to it? Lucan imagined him manhandling the bottom into it, and an uncomfortable feeling cooled his insides.

But Court wouldn't do that, would he? He'd find someone like Lucan who was into having sex at the end of a scene, or during one.

Lucan picked up his phone and cradled it over his lap like a grenade capable of causing untold damage. *You still mess me up after all this time*, Court had said last night. And the words had affected Lucan more than he'd thought they ever could, making his skin prickle and his heart lift. After all these years, the feelings were still there, buried and fragile. Lucan knew, even though he'd never want to admit it out loud, that if he let Court get any closer, they could be a *thing* again. Lucan could be that needy, twitchy little sub who couldn't get enough of his Dominant. Or maybe it would just be some stupid bullshit that went nowhere, but it was still dangerous. That was why Lucan had been so mean—not that he'd really thought before he'd sent that text. He looked at it now.

Not my problem. And I don't care. Now leave me alone

Court hadn't texted anything back; Lucan had probably hurt him. A mixture of guilt and satisfaction welled up in him at the thought. How many times had Lucan needed Court only to find he was getting drunk at the frat house? Lucan had been curled up in his bed at least a handful of times, aching all over where Court had bruised him with his rough hands or welted him with his belt, needing reassurance that Court gave a shit, that he only hurt Lucan because they both liked it. Every time, Court had been busy avoiding him. At least, that was what it had felt like to Lucan.

Lucan wanted to scream, but he had to settle for tensing up all his muscles and imagining the sound wailing from his throat. If he went primal-scream crazy in his room right now, his roommates would come running. Dom might even mention getting Lucan *help*, but Lucan had had therapy before—after breaking up with Court.

Fuck Court for bringing all these memories back to the surface. Lucan couldn't control his fingers as they furiously typed out a text. *Do you even know what aftercare is? Have you ever cuddled with anyone in your goddamn life? Just sleeping in the same bed isn't cuddling!*

Lucan felt a little like he'd felt before getting on meds for his depression: completely aware of the fact that other people would find his behavior wacked but at the same time, completely unable to translate his words into something rational. He couldn't be rational where Court was concerned. He couldn't be sane in relationships at all; he was either a mess like this or shut-up like a pill bug terrified to have its tender parts exposed. This was why he didn't date anymore, why he only did nonsexual kink scenes and had friends he never *ever* hooked up with.

Unable to face whatever Court's response to his overemotional text would be, Lucan shoved his phone under his pillow and curled up into a ball.

* * *

The adrenaline was wearing off by now, but Court was still a little jumpy. Even though he'd been working as an emergency medical technician for a few years now, it still gave him a rush to come off a string of intense calls. Tonight, he and his paramedic partner, Rosamie, had headed out to the scenes of three separate car accidents. It wasn't anything like joy Court had felt stopping that bleeding and setting those bones, but the adrenaline had given him a nice kick.

Now, he and Rosamie had just come back from transporting some patients to UPMC Mercy. As he shut the door of his locker at the EMS facility, he wasn't nearly tired yet. Maybe he'd be crashing now if he'd been on a twelve- or 24-hour shift, but the City of Pittsburgh had recently instituted eight-hour shifts for EMTs. The change was what had allowed Court to finally get his feet wet in the local kink scene.

He powered up his cell phone, which had been sitting in his locker since 3:00 p.m. After bidding goodbye to Rosamie, he headed out to the parking lot. On his way, he swiped the pattern to unlock his phone. A bunch of notifications appeared: a few emails, a missed call from his mom and an accompanying text (*Just wanted to chat. Love you*). Then there was a text from Lucan.

Seeing Lucan's name in the stark-white sans serif lit up Court's nerves with fresh excitement.

Do you even know what aftercare is? Have you ever cuddled with anyone in your goddamn life? Just sleeping in the same bed isn't cuddling!

Court heard the text in Lucan's strung-out voice, and he found himself grinning even as nausea bit at his stomach. He didn't know what in the hell Lucan was talking about, but he was talking; that was all that mattered.

Court got into his black sedan.

This text wasn't like the texts from last night but more like the old Lucan. When they'd dated, he'd used to send Court so many texts that were just fucked-up puzzles, niggling Court's brain like song lyrics or a name he couldn't remember, except the stakes were much higher if he didn't succeed. A prime example was the one Lucan had sent ending things: *I just can't do this anymore. You don't care about me. It's over.* As if Court had ever cared so much about anyone or anything. Court had failed to solve that last puzzle because Lucan had refused to give him any clues.

Now, Court didn't even try to make sense of Lucan's words; he knew it was hopeless. Instead, he sent *What are you talking about?* It was only while waiting for an answer that he realized Lucan's initial text was from hours ago. Oh, well. Lucan would just have to realize that Court had an important job. EMTs in some places sat around all the time waiting for emergencies, but in Pittsburgh, it was go-go-go almost all the time, especially when his shift covered rush hour.

Lucan wouldn't know he was an EMT, though. When they'd been together, Court had talked about maybe changing his major, but Lucan hadn't been around when Court dropped out of school. Of course, he'd gone back to get his EMT certificate, but that was later.

Before starting his car, Court sent another text. *Was at work all day, sorry. Personal phones have to be locked up.*

It wasn't until he was home at his apartment, closing and locking the door as quietly as possible so as not to wake Cally, his twin sister and roommate, that his phone buzzed in the pocket of his thick uniform pants. In his bedroom, he bent down to quickly free his sweaty feet from the confines of his boots before checking the notification.

Lucan had texted a simple *It's cool.*

Wow, Lucan had changed! Where was the novel about everything Court had done wrong to make Lucan text him in the first place? Maybe this was better for Lucan; a two-word text was less messy. But Court deserved an explanation, and he was damn well going to get one.

Tell me what you were talking about, he said.

It doesn't matter now. I'm over it

Court snarled. He'd much rather argue than have Lucan shut him down. *I've cuddled. We used to.*

Only whenever you made me binge watch Grey's Anatomy.

Now that was a nice memory: Lucan attached to Court's side, hands curled around Court's arm like a lemur's paws on a branch. Every once in a while, Lucan's soft lips would press to the side of Court's neck.

I still watch that, Court said.

I bet you do

Maybe it was Court reading into things, but the text didn't feel friendly. Lucan had used to tease Court at the ends of the most emotionally brutal episodes of the show. Court had never cried, but he got prickly, irritable, wanted sex. An orgasm after an episode of *Grey's* was a simple, perfect type of pleasure, and Lucan had been the best man for the job. Plus, he couldn't make fun of Court if he had a dick in his mouth.

Court stripped and got into the shower. He couldn't hear the phone vibrate over the sounds from the water pounding the shower walls. When he got out, he barely dried his hands before picking it up again to check.

Nothing. He had to say something else, or the conversation was going to die. *I do know what aftercare is.*

Did Google teach you?

He'd heard the term at a munch, but was that really relevant? *Why did you ask me if I knew?*

I looked at your FetNet profile.

And?

Lucan sent an angry emoji along with *It made me remember how much you sucked at it*

Still dripping wet and making two growing dark spots in Cally's fancy memory-foam bath rug, Court had the sudden urge to make someone's skin red—Lucan's. It had been way too long since he'd gotten to spank someone hard. If he found somebody on a hookup app, they were always saying things like "That's a little rough, man," and "The spanking's cool, but can you put your dick in me already?" But Court knew Lucan liked it hard.

Read me the riot act, Luc, he said. *You know it gets me off.*

Fuck you.

The text warmed Court more than his hot shower had. *You're bitchy tonight. How long has it been since someone turned you out? Your boyfriend not giving you what you need?*

Court had time to dry off and put on his boxers before Lucan answered him.

You don't know what I need.

Yes I do. Better than anyone. Or have you forgotten?

Fuck off.

You need a good beating at least twice a week or you start getting antsy and trying to call shots. But a little rough treatment and you get so precious, Luc. Sweet. Court sent the text without thinking, and there was another delay. Had he gone too far? He got into bed with his phone resting next to his head, nervous energy compelling him to pick at his cuticles until one of them bled.

Buzz, buzz, went Court's phone.

Dom isn't my boyfriend. He's my play partner.

Play partner was another term Court had learned because of a munch. It was the person you did a scene with, but Lucan probably meant Dom was a regular partner. They'd looked pretty chummy on that couch anyway.

But Dom wasn't Lucan's boyfriend. That was all that mattered.

Lucan sent another text: *Dom takes care of me. He doesn't hit me. I don't need that shit to function.* And another: *You DON'T know what I need. You don't know anything about me anymore. You don't know shit, Court!*

Okay, okay, Court typed frantically. *Sorry for whatever I did.* Ten minutes later, he added, *Lucan, really. I'm sorry. Why are you so upset about aftercare and cuddling suddenly? Just explain it to me!* But an hour later still, as Court's limbs and eyelids finally got heavy, Lucan still hadn't responded.

CHAPTER 4

WITH HIS BEDROOM door closed to expose the full-length mirror on the back, Lucan tried on shirt after shirt trying to find the perfect one. He had considered not going to the party tonight, but until he and his roommates got their shit together and hosted their own, there were only two per month that Lucan felt comfortable going to: last week's TNG party and tonight's semi-public one, Deviant Pleasures.

Unfortunately, according to the event listing on FetNet, Court was going to be there.

Oh, well. Humiliation over those overemotional texts licked Lucan's insides like a dead pet come back to life, but Lucan wasn't going to let Court's reappearance make him hibernate. Lucan had gone through a few rough spells where he didn't go to any parties, but that was before he'd moved in with Dom, Roland, and Erin. He wasn't going to disappear on people anymore, and he definitely wasn't going to miss out on playing with Dom. He could schedule a private play session with him, but the idea of private play made Lucan jumpy in a bad way. Too intimate.

He should never have texted Court like he had. But it had happened, and it was nothing Lucan hadn't done before. The difference now was that he wasn't going to wallow in his embarrassment for like a week over it.

He settled on a T-shirt made of teal mesh. Paired with ripped skinny jeans, the outfit was just trashy enough. The official story was that he hated that Court was going to be at the party, but the sad, twisted, and true one was that he hoped Court noticed him, thought he looked hot. Last night...

Lucan turned away from his own reflection. Last night, he'd gotten off to the fantasy of Court grabbing him again and manhandling him into the venue's bathroom. Lucan wouldn't let him get away with much, maybe a little kissing, some dry humping. And Court would whine desperately because he couldn't have what he wanted.

It was just a fantasy. Court would never act like that, never submit to the will of a sub. Some BDSM rookies never could get it into their heads that it was the bottom who called the shots at the end of the day. They *let* the Top get away with things.

Court would be one of those clueless rookies. He'd fuck up badly enough at some party and get himself kicked out, and word would get around, and he'd be barred everywhere. It was only a matter of time.

"Y'all ready?" came Roland's booming yell.

Lucan made his way outside to Roland's van along with Dom and Erin. Erin had gone full babygirl with her sandy hair in bouncy pigtails and a sucker in her mouth. Her tiny denim shorts were much more appropriate for the muggy summer air than Lucan's jeans, but Lucan would end up in his underwear before the night was through. Dom opened the trunk and set his play bag inside.

Dressed in a brown leather jacket and suave sunglasses, Roland opened the passenger's-side door and said, "Come sit next to Daddy, babygirl."

Lucan and Dom got into the back seat.

Dom chuckled. "How does Ro pull off that pedophile look so damn well?"

From the front seat, Roland flipped Dom the bird. Lucan just rolled his eyes.

Fifteen minutes later, Roland was parking the van behind the biker bar where Deviant Pleasures was held. As far as Lucan knew, the bikers themselves weren't involved in the lifestyle, but they were comfortable with having kinksters as paying guests in their space. The venue was closed to the public for the party with some of the bikers working as bouncers and bartenders.

Lucan and his roommates each handed their twenty-dollar tribute to the guy at the door. Immediately afterward, Lucan scanned the room for Court. The area held several sets of tables and chairs with ten or so people chatting, and a handful of partygoers sat at the bar. Next to the bar was the door to the playroom, the dungeon's dark walls visible and a faint bass beat thumping from its wide entrance.

Maybe Court was in there? He probably had his eyes glued to whoever was scening. Though he was experienced in private kink with Lucan—and who knew who else he'd screwed since then?—he was probably still getting used to seeing people play with an audience. There was full nudity and sex allowed at Deviant Pleasures, though the guests rarely went that far.

Holding his bag, Dom came up to Lucan's side. "When were you wanting to scene?"

Lucan chewed on his lip. "Maybe in an hour?"

"Okay."

Roland and Erin were going over to a table, and Roland had Erin's turquoise box of coloring supplies in hand. Before they sat down, Roland pulled a small stuffed animal out of his coat, and Erin squealed.

Lucan glanced over at the bar where a muscled guy in a leather biker's vest was pouring someone a coke. Lucan ached for a drink to calm his nerves, but it was irresponsible to have alcohol before scening, even if he and Dom weren't going to do it right away. Best to wait until after.

He headed into the playroom. *Home*, his soul whispered. Black floor mats gleamed under unobtrusive lighting that lent a glow to the skin in the room. A dark-skinned submissive looked particularly beautiful contorted and wiggling in a hog tie as her femme Top giggled and tapped the bottoms of her feet with a cane. Another couple occupied the spanking bench. As it was still early, two out of three bondage frames stood empty, but near the third one, a small group gathered. One of the party was Court.

Lucan's mouth went dry. Court was wearing leather pants and nothing else, and red scratches streaked his back. At the end of his perfectly sculpted arm a metal object glinted—one of those cooking tools used to separate pulled pork. A meat claw? Griffin, the Dungeon Master from the last party, had another of the tools in his hand. He must have shown Court what they felt like.

The thought of Court submitting to pain of any kind was strange, but it was always a good idea for a Top to feel a sensation before inflicting it on a bottom.

Unable to control his feet, Lucan stepped closer.

"You'd be surprised what treasures you can find in the supermarket," Griffin was saying, and his round belly shook when he laughed.

Court handed him the meat claw.

"Giving Court some tips?" Lucan asked. He didn't mean to speak, but again, it was as if he couldn't control himself. He was too warm, his chest too tight.

Court looked at him, his eyes crinkling as his lips spread into a smile. "Hey."

"Hey," Lucan said.

Nobody had ever been happy to see Lucan after they'd been on the receiving end of his crazy texts. Only Court. It was a prime example of why they were awful together.

Court showed Lucan his back. "How is it?"

The scratches were barely visible now. "He went easy on you." Seeing the muscles under the smooth skin, Lucan sympathized with Court's desire to touch without asking. The difference was he'd never act on it.

Griffin said, "Have you started building a toy bag, Court?"

"I have a few things," Court said.

"Like what?" asked Lucan.

Court gave him a look of pure heat. "Stuff you'd like." He leaned close and whispered into Lucan's ear, "Can we talk somewhere?" He was near enough for Lucan to feel his warmth, but he didn't put his hands on him.

Still, Griffin gave Lucan a look that asked if he should intervene.

Lucan shouldn't go anywhere with Court; Court didn't honor boundaries. But the pull was like quicksand, or like spirits come up from a dark dimension to yank Lucan down. And Court wasn't fundamentally a bad guy or anything. If he did something and Lucan wanted him to stop, he would as long as Lucan was adamant enough.

"Okay," he whispered.

Court pulled back and gestured for Lucan to take the lead. Where should they go? Lucan's thoughts moved too fast for him to follow, but his feet took control again, taking him and Court out of the bar altogether and outside into the sticky heat.

He stalled a few feet from a group of smokers, his heart thudding down to his toes.

"My car?" Court asked. If he was nervous, he didn't show it, but Lucan couldn't remember ever seeing Court shaken up. Angry, sure, but not scared.

"Yeah." Lucan followed Court across the parking lot, the light from various lamps reflecting off the smooth parts of the pavement and Court's leather pants.

They stopped next to a black sedan. There were lots of cars around, but no people.

Lucan opened his mouth to speak, but before he could get a sound out, Court rounded on him, pushing him back-first against the car door, then framing him with his perfect, bare arms. All that skin, so close but no longer touching as Court used his body as a cage.

Lucan's stomach churned in fear and delight.

"Tell me what you meant the other night. When you were texting me about cuddling and aftercare. Why were you so pissed at me?" The blunt words and Court's stormy eyes held all of Lucan's attention. This wasn't anything like Lucan's fantasy, where Lucan held Court back and Court whined in frustration, but Lucan knew better than to think Court would ever give him power like that.

Lucan thought about turning away, but there was nowhere to go. Just hard metal and Court's hard body, and if Lucan moved just a little, he'd touch it. Him. The danger.

"Forget it," Lucan managed.

"No." A squeak to Lucan's left—Court was clenching his fingers against the car, and he shifted almost imperceptibly closer. "We're not doing that. You don't get to confuse me with your bullshit and then cut me off when I ask for an explanation. I'm not young and stupid anymore."

A memory, another one—Court pushing Lucan against the wall at his frat house, knee between Lucan's legs. "I give the orders, you obey them. I ask questions, you answer them. It's not that fucking deep, baby."

Lucan was sweltering and chilled at the same time. Could he have Court's knee now? A little pressure between his legs would feel so good.

Court slapped the body of the car, making Lucan jump. "If you don't give me an explanation right fucking now..."

"I wasn't in my right mind when I sent that text, Court! It doesn't matter. I'm over it. I don't want to talk about it."

Court showed his teeth and stared Lucan down. "We're not going back inside until you talk about it."

Lucan glanced past Court. From here, he could see the smokers they'd passed, but it was as if those people were in another world. Still, Lucan could make this stop if he wanted. He could get loud and angry and kick and shove—make Court understand that he truly didn't want this. But being trapped under Court's scrutiny felt more like home than any dungeon.

Time moved slowly under the weight of Court's silence and unforgiving gaze. Eventually, Lucan's lips and tongue couldn't take it anymore.

"You want to know what I was talking about?" Heat licked Lucan's cheeks. "What I was thinking about when I sent that text?" *Don't say it, don't say it*— "You were a shitty Dom, okay? You didn't give me aftercare. I was looking at your stupid FetNet profile and you had that stupid kink listed, 'cuddling as aftercare,' and I just fucking snapped. You're full of shit. You aren't into that at all!" Lucan's whole head burned, and he squeezed his hands into fists.

Between Court's brows, a deep wrinkle appeared. "Says who?"

"Says me!" Lucan pushed Court with both hands, and Court leaned into the touch, the pressure keeping Lucan's palms snugly against the warm, naked skin. "Let me go," Lucan whispered.

"But you don't want me to." Court gripped Lucan's wrists and forced them down. "You love being under me." His eyes fell half-closed; he must be getting Top-high from this.

The submissive in Lucan responded. Heat spread through him like his body was preparing for a porn shoot or something. He hadn't been touched in years, and he wanted Court to be the one to do it—touch him, hurt him, make him lose control. *Use me. I'm yours.*

Lucan made a half-hearted attempt to pull free, testing his bonds, and Court forced Lucan's hands behind his back and pressed against him, his lips finding his cheek. "I'll cuddle you after I play with you. Promise." He spoke against Lucan's skin so that he felt every word—the vibrations and breath.

Lucan was so hard he wanted to scream. Unable to use his hands, he nuzzled Court. "Promise... Promise you won't hurt me."

"You like when it hurts."

"Not like that. Please." Lucan's stupid mouth. Why did he have to beg? Why did it feel so good to beg?

"Shh." Court loosened his grip on Lucan's wrist and slid his hand down, aligned their palms, intertwined their fingers. "I got you. Don't be scared." With his other hand, he held the back of Lucan's neck and pressed a kiss to his forehead.

Lucan didn't care that Court's skin was sticky against his own. The inherently dominant gesture and those confident, comforting words touched him in his most sensitive places. "Please." Begging again. So pathetic.

Court pulled back enough to meet Lucan's gaze. His eyes were dark pits. "Please what, baby?"

"I don't know." Lucan swallowed with a dry throat. "Keep going." *Please, please, please—*

Court chuckled, the sound arrogant and musical, and stepped back. "I will. Get in the car."

What? Oh. Lucan had to move. He turned and fumbled for the door handle before yanking the door open and crawling into the back seat.

He got situated on the far side. How uncomfortable this cramped, hot space would be barely registered as all of Lucan's senses became consumed with what he wanted, where he was about to be touched, Court crawling in with him and pulling the door shut and undoing his pants.

What was going to happen now? What was Court going to do to him?

Court had a little trouble getting his leather pants off, and Lucan only barely managed not to laugh.

"You look good in them at least," he said.

Court gave Lucan a playful look. "Shut up and get over here."

It was as if Lucan had never had sex in his life. He was so awkward crawling onto Court's lap and trying to undo his own jeans like he'd never seen a button. But it was just that he couldn't stop looking at the shape of Court's cock inside his underwear long enough to worry about his own dick.

"Are you gonna take those off, too?" he asked shyly and gestured at Court's briefs.

"You first." Court nudged Lucan's hands away and undid Lucan's fly himself. He yanked his jeans down, exposing boxers. Lucan had wanted to be comfortable tonight when he scened, but the cotton fabric made the wet spot he'd leaked obvious.

Court rubbed his thumb in the moisture, touching Lucan's cockhead in the process.

Lucan held back a whimper, shifting back and meeting resistance in the form of the front seat's rigid back. "Stop torturing me."

Court chuckled. "Oh, please. You know what torture is, and this isn't it." Finally, he pushed down his briefs, exposing a thick, familiar cock with an unfamiliar dydoe piercing.

A wave of violent arousal hit Lucan. "That's so hot. Court..." At the base of Court's cockhead, a silver ball glinted in the light from a streetlamp outside the car window. Gently, Lucan nudged it with his thumb.

Court touched the tiny black ring in Lucan's septum. "So's this. Cute."

"Thanks." Lucan couldn't help but smile at the compliment.

Court ran his fingers through Lucan's hair, pushing back the dyed-blond strands. For a second, Lucan thought he might kiss him, but instead, he suspended his palm below Lucan's mouth.

"Spit," he said.

The unexpected command had Lucan hesitating. But it was clear why Court had asked, so Lucan did as told.

"I need more than that," Court said. "Drool for me."

Embarrassment made Lucan's cheeks hotter than they already were. He did *not* like talking about bodily functions or being ordered to perform them. But it was just spit. Lube.

He pooled saliva in his mouth and spit it into Court's palm.

"Good boy," said Court.

Lucan's cock pulsed in response to the praise. He needed Court to touch him, please, *now*.

Court wrapped his big hand around both their cocks and pumped. *Yes.* The jewelry in Court's piercing added another dimension to the friction, rubbing against Lucan's sensitive skin and teasing his nerves.

Court moved his hand away, leaving Lucan to helplessly rut, but then he was yanking the fabric scrunched at Lucan's lower back farther down, exposing more of his ass. With his other hand, he delivered a stinging slap.

Lucan yelped, then moaned as the pain bloomed. Nails digging into Court's shoulders, he arched his back to make his ass easier to reach and silently begged for more pain.

Court gave him another hit. He picked up a ruthless rhythm with no warm-up, but Lucan didn't mind. He loved the shock and fear of being helpless to intense sensations, and though these weren't necessarily pleasant, they scratched an itch—one that Lucan had been carrying around so long he'd almost forgotten to take care of it. Hit after hit after hit rained down, on one side and then the other as Court switched hands.

Lucan worked his hips until a sweat broke out, and his cock begged for release. But he couldn't get there. He was on the cusp, trapped in a wonderful hell, too restricted by his clothing that wasn't all the way off but too single-minded to do anything about it.

The ruthless hits to his ass stopped abruptly, and Court growled like an animal. Lucan cried out as the pain in his ass intensified; no longer drowned out by unbroken stimulation, the skin throbbed, angry.

Court stuck two burning-hot fingers into Lucan's mouth. With no hesitation this time, Lucan coated them in as much drool as he could muster. Then Court found Lucan's hole and pushed his fingers in.

Lucan moaned loud from a parched throat. His hole clenched involuntarily at the intrusion, but Court shoved despite the bit of resistance. The sheer dominance of the act, the force, the burn... They brought Lucan impossibly close to the edge. Just one more shove of Court's fingers, and he would—

Court gripped the base of Lucan's cock and staved off the orgasm.

"No," Lucan moaned, slapping Court's shoulders. "Please!"

Court remained a wordless tormentor, shoving until he got deep enough to hit Lucan's prostate. Then he stayed there, massaging and massaging, drowning Lucan in sensation. Lucan had no choice then but to give in to the onslaught, and his spine curved as he bent over Court, rubbing his face on the soft felt fabric of the car's interior behind Court's head.

"Good boy," said Court, his voice strained.

Lucan whimpered. He needed to empty his balls so badly, but Court kept his orgasm just out of reach with that painful grip on his dick, building and building the pressure in Lucan's groin but giving it nowhere to go.

After a while—Lucan didn't know how long—Court withdrew his fingers and let go of Lucan's cock. Lucan choked on air. His cock twitched helplessly but still didn't shoot, and Court ran his hands up and down Lucan's back, shushing and soothing.

Then he yanked Lucan's head up by the hair and once more had him produce drool. Lucan was like a marionette now, whittled down and given over to Court's whims. It no longer embarrassed him to spit.

When Court took them in hand again, his strokes were torturously slow. He was doing it to himself, too, barely giving their swollen cocks enough friction for—for anything. That piercing rubbed in the most awful way, making Lucan shudder but not pushing him high enough. He needed more. More sensation, more anything.

"Look at me," said Court.

Lucan registered that he'd been staring at their cocks in Court's hand and tore his eyes away to focus on Court's dark gaze instead. "I need to come." He rubbed his forehead against the top of Court's head.

"I know. I got you." Court began pumping in earnest.

Desperate and ruined, Lucan thrust into Court's grip erratically, mindlessly, like an animal. And Court made low, guttural noises, a beast in frat boy skin. As they slithered together faster, Court punctuated every beat with a growl. Then cum hit Lucan's neck— Court's cum.

Court let go of their cocks. Lucan's twitched once, twice, still didn't squirt. He needed pain! He needed it to come, and Court knew it, but he wasn't giving it to him.

"Fuck you." Lucan really hurt Court this time, digging deep scratches into his arms.

Court seemed impervious to the pain. "Mad at me, baby?"

"I hate you." The thick, pained words weren't only about Lucan's need to come. "Hate what you do to me. You don't 'got' me, Court. You don't, you don't."

"Yes, I do." Court took Lucan's head and locked eyes with him. "Before you leave this car, you're going to come. Have I ever left you hanging?"

Hot tears escaped from the corners of Lucan's eyes, but he shook his head. Court had never not made him come; he could admit that.

"That's right." Court tapped Lucan on the nose. "You're worried for nothing." Court moved, and a second later, Lucan was face-first over Court's lap. Court bent his arms behind his back and held his wrists in a firm but comfortable grip. With his free hand, he shoved Lucan's jeans down to his knees.

Lucan moaned before Court even touched his ass because he knew what was coming: more spanking.

"You can come at any time, but it has to be from this." Court massaged Lucan's ass cheeks; the tenderness from the earlier spanking was almost gone already. "I'll hit you all night if I have to."

Such a thing would be dangerous, but Lucan wouldn't last that long. Not when he'd denied himself this type of play.

"Is that understood, babe?" Court asked.

"Yes."

"Yes, what?"

Lucan's stomach clenched. He shouldn't say it, shouldn't go there. Court wasn't his Dominant—not anymore. They didn't have any type of arrangement, and Lucan didn't give honorifics away to just anyone. But Court wasn't just anyone, was he? And Lucan couldn't stop the ill-advised word. It rioted behind his lips and teeth, then finally broke through. "Yes, Sir." With it came the sweetest defeat; Lucan fell swiftly into subspace, all his muscles going slack as his mind surrendered to Court's plan.

"Good boy." Court stroked his hair. "Now let me get you there." He started the spanking.

At first, each hit was decipherable: impact, sting. But as Court kept going, Lucan experienced the pain as warmth spreading over his whole consciousness. He floated within it, on top of it, through it. He went to another place, watched himself being hit, watched Court's arm muscles straining as he pounded and pounded, watched them together in Lucan's dorm room during Lucan's first ever spanking. Back then, the act itself had been enough to melt his brain, and he'd come so fast.

"Did you really just come on my jeans?" Court had asked. "Gross, babe. Well, I'm not finished yet." *Slap.* "This feels too"—*slap*—"fucking"—*slap*—"good."

"That's it," said the current Court, and Lucan remembered suddenly that he had lungs. As Court spanked him harder than he'd ever been spanked before without an implement, it was nearly impossible for him to get enough air. Someone who wasn't a masochist would probably be suffering right now, but Lucan was on the edge of bliss.

"It's time for you to come. Don't—" Court hissed. "—fight it."

Lucan was beyond fighting it. He was nothing but a passive receiver of the things Court was doing to him. Court could do anything right now, absolutely anything, and Lucan would silently thank him for it and beg him to do it again. He had forgotten his lungs again, but now he remembered his groin. It seemed that part of him was bigger than the rest, the tension there building and building and—

Lucan's whole body tensed as his balls constricted, pushing cum out his overswollen cock. The orgasm hit him like a beating. When it was over, he lay empty and exhausted as if he'd just done hours of physical labor.

Slowly—very slowly—he returned to reality. He registered the fabric of the car's interior under his head, the fog on the window, the sweaty stickiness wherever his skin touched Court's. His mesh shirt sat raked up his back, his jeans and underwear bunched around his lower half. Court was taking deep, noisy breaths punctuated with little whimpers.

Lucan blinked. Whimpers? Out of *Court*?

Gingerly, Lucan crawled off Court. When he finally managed to get his ass in the seat, he regretted it. The skin was beyond tender, and pulling up his pants and underwear was a rare type of torture that he didn't quite get off on.

Court stopped panting like he'd just run a marathon, but he didn't move to cover his limp cock. He was holding out a shaky right hand.

Lucan gently took it in his own. "Hurt yourself?"

"Yeah. Should have brought my gloves."

Still swimming in his submissive headspace, Lucan pressed the lightest of kisses to the reddened palm.

Court made a low sound. "Maybe I'll never wear gloves if you kiss it better every time."

An uncomfortable feeling niggled at the back of Lucan's head. *Every time...* Court talked as if this was going to happen again and again.

Lucan was too endorphin-drunk to deal with that, so he pushed the thought away. He helped Court pull up his underwear and those hot but impractical leather pants.

That was when the awkward silence descended. Lucan felt a little ill; his body wasn't used to all this. He opened the car door just to feel some airflow. Fuck, it was hot. He needed water. He needed—

Shit. "I was supposed to scene with Dom." The realization hit him hard, and his ill feeling intensified. No way he could scene with Dom now. And they'd had an agreement, a plan. Fuck, this was so rude of him!

"What's the matter?" asked Court.

"I was supposed to *scene* with *Dom*. Not you." And Dom was not the type to let this go. Lucan needed to get ahead of it, find Dom and explain.

He moved to get out of the car.

Court held him back with a grip on his arm. Always with the grabbing!

"I thought we were going to cuddle," he said.

Eyes on the parking lot, Lucan replied, "I can't right now."

"You're just going to run away? Fuck that!"

Lucan yanked his arm free. "Give me a minute to talk to Dom. Is that too much to ask?"

Court waved his hand in an angry, dismissive gesture.

Lucan got shakily to his feet. He was embarrassingly out of it, but this couldn't wait until the high passed, which could be hours from now. Court had hurt him so good, but Lucan was still an idiot. This was *Court*. The scene had been too intense for sub drop not to hit, so a day or two from now, when Lucan was a crying mess, Court would conveniently not get Lucan's texts or be out fucking around with whatever asshole friends he kept these days.

Inside the venue, the lights were much too bright. Squinting, Lucan found Dom at the bar drinking a soda.

It only took Dom a few seconds of taking in Lucan's appearance to know exactly what had happened. Lucan could see the recognition dawn on his face. "Seriously?" he asked, gaze sharp and glinting.

Lucan pushed back his sweaty bangs. There was no point in trying to talk around the truth because subspace was obvious in the dazed demeanor and blown pupils that Lucan was positive he possessed right now. "Yeah. I'm really sorry. I know it's inexcusable."

CHAPTER 5

COURT WOULDN'T LIE; he felt a little fucking used. Hand stinging, fly open, skin sticky with sweat, he wanted to slap Lucan once more for leaving him alone. Especially since he'd done it to talk to Dom. Court was the only Dom Lucan needed to be worrying about right now—the one who'd given him what he'd needed, what he'd been begging for with every whimper, shiver, and whine.

Truly, Court had just wanted to talk tonight. Get some answers. He tried to remember what Lucan had told him about those texts, but the haze of his afterglow was too strong. He'd gotten Lucan alone, and he'd just...lost it.

Not that he had a single real regret. He didn't even mind the scratches smarting on his arms that Lucan had dug into him in the throes of need. Court loved them, actually. Lucan was like that—spiky, dangerous. Court loved controlling that vicious energy, turning it into *pleases* and *noes* and *yeses* all focused on him and the pleasure and pain he was doling out.

He'd prefer to have Lucan still here with him. The main reason he hadn't made it easy for Lucan to come was because he hadn't wanted their time together to end. But as he sat staring at the back of the driver's seat, he remembered what Lucan had said. That Court wasn't into cuddling, that he hadn't given Lucan aftercare, that he'd been a bad Dom.

A bad Dom. Well, Court couldn't remember Lucan ever complaining.

And yeah, he wasn't much for cuddling after a hookup, but this was Lucan. A desperate need to keep him close simmered in Court's core. That little kiss to Court's tender palm had been nice but not enough.

Court's afterglow faded into defensive anger that energized him to move. Screw Lucan's "I need a minute to talk to another guy." Court needed a minute! Of Lucan's time. But first, he pried his phone out of the impossibly snug pocket of his leather pants and did a quick Google search for the word "aftercare." He was familiar with the concept, but he wanted to be sure.

In BDSM, the period immediately after a scene in which either the Dominant or submissive partner (or both) receives physical and/or psychological care, which often includes cuddling or a discussion about the scene.

Ha! Had Court not just tried to do that? Growling, he got out of the car and headed back toward the bar. Lucan had better be in there. If he couldn't find him, Court would blow up his phone until he did.

Court burst back into the party. The person at the door tried to stop him, but he just waved and said, "I've already paid. MisterK289, black Toyota Camry." Lucan's voice coming from the bar alerted Court to Lucan and Dom's location. They were clearly in the middle of an argument, and an urge to defend Lucan flared.

Court advanced with his face hard and his arms crossed.

"Please try to understand," Lucan was saying. "It wasn't planned!"

"You talking about me?" Court asked, even though he knew they were.

Lucan's gaze was cutting when it landed on Court. "Did I not say I needed a minute?"

Court scowled. "Minute's up."

"Wow," Dom muttered. He pointed squarely at Lucan. "You disrespected me tonight."

"I'm fucking sorry, Dom," said Lucan. But Dom was walking off, and he disappeared into the room with all the kink equipment.

Court tapped Lucan's shoulder so he'd have his full attention. "We're going back to the car."

Lucan sighed dramatically. "Can we go somewhere else? It's fucking hot out there."

"Like where?"

"My house?" Lucan bit his lip. "No one's there right now."

At the suggestion—and that cute little lip bite—Court's anger almost disappeared. Almost. "Sure."

Lucan got a lost look in the eyes, so Court put a hand on the small of his back and led him to the parking lot. They were quiet all the way to the car; then Lucan had to tell Court his address.

As they drove, Lucan tapped annoyingly on the center console.

Court grabbed his hand and held it still. "Don't worry, Dom will forgive you."

"No offense, but you don't know anything about Dom and his grudges."

"Okay, well, you already apologized. Nothing else you can do about it now."

"I guess." Lucan took his hand away.

"How's your ass feeling?" Court asked.

"Not great."

"If you have something with aloe in it—"

"I know how to take care of a spanked ass, Court."

Lucan's interruption—and his tone—had Court's anger from earlier coming back. He was only trying to take care of Lucan. Why was he getting this attitude? "There's no reason to be bitchy with me."

"No reason? I can think of a few."

Court clenched his jaw so hard it popped. What the fuck had he done now? "What are you talking about?"

"What happened between us tonight. None of that was okay."

Court only barely managed not to miss the next turn. He felt like a cartoon character, red-faced with steam coming out of his ears. "Oh, yeah, I'm the bad guy. I gave you a great orgasm and then wanted to cuddle you. How can I be such an asshole?"

"You pushed me into it. You didn't ask for consent. And you hit me without making sure I was okay with that."

Oh my God. Was Lucan serious right now? "You loved it!"

"You aren't getting it, Court! You aren't fucking listening to me!"

Oh, he was listening. It was just that nothing Lucan was saying was making any goddamn sense. Overwhelmed, Court opted for stony silence and was relieved when Lucan went quiet, too. At Lucan's place, he put the car in Park and waited for him to get out.

"Are you not coming?" Lucan's tone was pitiful, but that shit didn't penetrate Court's cold armor.

"Why should I? You're set on making me the enemy."

"Don't be dramatic. That's not what this is."

Court locked gazes with Lucan. "Then what is it?"

After a few tense seconds, Lucan smirked. "I need you to come put aloe on my ass."

The words broke down some of the tightness in Court's muscles. And who was he kidding anyway? He wasn't going to leave if Lucan didn't want him to, no matter how pissed off he was.

He rolled his eyes and got out of the car, then followed Lucan into the two-story house. Nightlights in various outlets illuminated their path to what Court assumed was Lucan's bedroom.

Lucan switched on the lamp on the nightstand. The place was a little messy with a few small piles of clothes on the floor and an unmade queen-sized bed. Quickly, Lucan untangled the sheets and comforter, and Court helped him make the surface more or less smooth.

"Do you want anything?" Lucan asked. "Water?"

"That'd be nice."

Lucan left and returned with two store-brand water bottles. Court unscrewed his and took a seat on the bed. "So." He took a long drink.

Standing an awkward few feet away, Lucan didn't open his bottle but instead tapped the plastic lid with his fingernails. Holy shit, that was a habit he would need to break.

"Come here," said Court.

"I think we should talk first."

Court set his water bottle on the nightstand. "We can't talk and cuddle at the same time?"

Lucan pursed his lips. "I don't think so."

"Okay, so what do we need to talk about?"

Lucan fidgeted and looked off to the side, and a deep flush spread over his pale throat. "I'm freaking out."

Court felt for him, but at the same time, he didn't really understand. What was there to freak out about? The sex had been great! Had Lucan not felt that? Had he not felt Court inside him? And Court wasn't talking about his fingers in his ass. "Why?"

"Because—" Lucan scratched up and down his arm. "You're going to hurt me again, and I'm so stupid. I'm so stupid, Court."

Jesus Christ. Court had been expecting another outburst, but this? Bringing up the past like *Lucan* had been the one who got dumped? "Stop acting like you didn't cut me loose with a fucking text message."

Lucan brought his gaze back, brows furrowed angrily. "I only did that because I wasn't getting what I needed from you!"

Court laughed. That was rich. "And just how was I supposed to know that?"

Lucan fidgeted some more and looked down at his hands. "If you're going to dominate somebody, you have to do research—"

"Research? I was just going on instinct." Court stood, feeling restless, agitated. Fear and guilt picked at him like vultures' beaks, but he'd been young. How was he supposed to have known this shit when Lucan was the first person he'd ever met with the same kinky urges? "I was doing what felt good. I wasn't trying to hurt you. I never left you afterward. I don't understand what you wanted me to do, Luc—"

"Aftercare isn't just for right after!" Lucan drifted closer, visibly shaking. "Sometimes the drop hits a couple days later, especially when the play is intense. Sometimes you *cut* me, Court. That's pretty fucking intense!"

Court swallowed hard, trying to keep his emotions under control. "Should I not have cut you?"

"No, but like... Days later, I needed you." Lucan took a breath and seemed to be having trouble keeping it together enough to speak. "You were always busy when we weren't together. Drinking, hanging out with the guys, studying, whatever. You wouldn't even answer a text. And I'd be in my fucking room bawling my eyes out having all these thoughts about—about how fucked-up I was for letting you do that shit to me and how you obviously didn't—didn't care except when I was ready to let you use me. You didn't— You didn't care." Lucan was crying now, choking on his words.

Court was afraid to touch him, like he was covered in an electric current. "I cared. I just needed... I needed breaks."

"Breaks." Lucan laughed mirthlessly and wiped at his cheeks.

"If I hadn't distanced myself, I would have failed out of school. I mean, I fucking failed anyway, but you were like a vacuum of desire. I had to be in you whenever I saw you." Just like now. Just like earlier. He sounded like such an idiot trying to explain it, though.

"A good Dom learns to control himself," said Lucan.

"I thought we already established I'm a shitty one," snapped Court.

Arms wrapped around himself, Lucan took another step closer. He sniffed. "Maybe just an uneducated one. I don't know. I just needed to tell you this. There's more, but I can't..." Lucan covered his face.

Court's body was a war zone as his emotions battled. Everything was tight and sick, and he hated it. Was he turned on, pissed off, sad, guilty, or...needy? "How long have you been doing this shit without me? Have you had guys cutting you?"

"No." Lucan shrugged his slender shoulders. "Four years or so?"

"Teach me." Court didn't know if that was what he really wanted or if he was only trying to find a way to have Lucan again no matter the cost to his pride. But the way things were going tonight... There wouldn't be any more hot fucks in parking lots if he wasn't careful. "If you know so damn much, teach me." *So I don't have to hear you accuse me of being awful ever again.*

Lucan's laugh this time was harsh and unpleasant.

"How does Dom do it to you?" Court asked. "Does he make you melt like I do?"

Lucan scoffed. "That's none of your business unless we play around you."

Court didn't like that *we*. "Be a good boy and tell me."

"Nah, you can't just pull that 'good boy' shit out of context."

"Tell me!"

"No. I'm not going to fucking tell you."

They stared at each other for long seconds, the only noise the short, sharp breaths through their noses. Lucan was raw, edgy, defiant—but he no longer looked like he was going to break. Part of Court wanted to back him into a corner and make him talk about every little thing he wasn't saying—about Dom, about BDSM, about all his little opinions of how Court had fucked up in the past or tonight or here, right now.

But Lucan's truths hurt, and Court didn't want to see him cry again.

"Go get that aloe shit," said Court.

Lucan broke eye contact but didn't move.

"Now!"

"Okay. Shit." Lucan disappeared into the hallway, and Court followed, hanging back a few feet. He would make damn sure Lucan was following his order.

Lucan went into a bathroom. When he came back out, he startled, eyes wide; apparently he hadn't expected to see Court just behind him.

"Here." He thrust a bottle at Court. The front of it proclaimed it held lotion with the required aloe in it.

"Thank you." Court led the way back to the bedroom. "Close the door and take off your clothes."

Lucan hesitated.

The beast inside Court—the one that liked to hit, hurt, praise, and punish—slithered and huffed. "This is aftercare, right? This is what you want?"

"Yeah, but..."

"What?"

Lucan opened his mouth, then closed it again. "I... I just feel so submissive, and I don't usually, and it's scary. Y-You made me call you 'Sir,' and we shouldn't have done that, Court. We shouldn't have done that."

Court narrowed his eyes. Slowly, he repeated, "Now you feel submissive."

Lucan nodded. Was the thing inside him a beast, too? Maybe. But Court pictured a tiny, shivering prey creature, needing to be hunted and fed upon and ruined. It only thought it was a beast when Court wasn't around.

"Strip, Lucan. All I'm going to do is put lotion on you."

Finally, Lucan obeyed. Court took off his pants as well because he wanted to be comfortable, but he kept his briefs on. He sat in the middle of the bed with his legs stretched out and patted his thigh. "Lie across me." Exhaustion hit him suddenly. The bed was soft; the house was warm. He hoped Lucan was going to let him sleep here.

Awkwardly, Lucan positioned himself across Court's lap. He was half-hard, but Court ignored it in favor of his rosy ass cheeks. He squirted some of the lotion onto them, and Lucan shivered, goose bumps rising all over him.

"You'll be fine in a day or two," said Court.

"Felt really hard at the time. You didn't give me a warm-up."

Gently, Court massaged the lotion into the soft skin. "Is that another callout?"

"No. I like it that way. Most people don't."

"I'm not spanking most people." Court snapped the lotion closed and set it on the nightstand next to his condensation-soaked water bottle.

Lucan crawled off him and sat next to Court on his knees, looking lost, like he needed to cross the street but there was no adult around to hold his hand.

"What now?" asked Court.

"I don't know."

"Tell me what you want."

"It's not about want. It's need." Lucan's cheeks were the most endearing pink when he asked, "Can we cuddle now?"

Court exhaled his relief. "Of course." He reached out and cupped Lucan's face. Immediately, Lucan pushed into the touch, his eyelids fluttering closed. The animal inside him must be purring.

"Adorable," Court whispered.

Lucan smirked. "Shut up." He put his boxers back on and plugged his phone into its charger. Court checked his phone as well, thinking it *might* make it until morning before the battery went dead. He had work tomorrow, but not until 3:00. Now, it wasn't even 11:30, and the whole house was still quiet.

"Am I sleeping here?" Court asked. "Or are we cuddling a little, then I leave?"

Lucan pulled the bedcovers back. "The second one."

Court was a little disappointed but not surprised. He was too tired to fight it. "All right."

They got into bed together. Court was the big spoon with Lucan pressed tightly against him, and Court breathed in the scent of Lucan's shampoo and rubbed his soft chest hair. He could go again. He wouldn't even need to order Lucan around, hurt him, or call him "good boy" to get off. They could just push their underwear down, and Court could slide his cock between those pretty cheeks and—

"I can feel you getting hard," Lucan said.

Court gave his head a shake as if to dispel the fantasy. "I didn't say anything about *your* dick when I was rubbing down your ass."

Lucan giggled. "True." He hugged Court's arm. "I just want to be held right now. Please don't push it, Court."

"I'm not pushing anything. I'm being good. I'm doing what you want. Need."

"Yeah." Lucan shifted but didn't let go of Court's arm. "You are. Thanks. Sorry," he added.

CHAPTER 6

A LOUD RINGING WOKE LUCAN. Shit, he'd fallen asleep. On the nightstand, the lamp was still on, and Lucan's phone shook, its screen lit, as it vibrated along with the ringing.

Court's solid warmth remained wrapped around Lucan, and he struggled to get out from under the heavy, muscled arm slung across him.

Court groaned and rubbed at his face.

Lucan reached for his phone, which bore Roland's name as the caller. "Hello?" His voice came out scratchy with sleep.

"Where the hell are you?" Roland's angry tone gave Lucan an anxious chill, bringing him to full alertness. The guy had a temper, and it was never a fun time to be on the receiving end of it, even if Roland's short fuse usually burned out quickly.

"Home. I got a ride from someone."

"Cool. Next time drop me a text so everybody's not worried about your ass, huh?"

"I'm sorry, Ro."

"Dom said you were with that ex of yours."

Lucan hated the guilt that pinched him. He winced. "Yeah."

"Thought you said he couldn't be trusted?"

Lucan swallowed. "Yeah, I said that."

"Well, I'm glad to hear you aren't off somewhere getting fucking hurt, dipshit!"

Lucan gripped his phone too tightly. "I fell asleep, asshole!"

But Roland had hung up.

Gritting his teeth, Lucan set his phone down a little too hard. Its screen remained illuminated, showing the time as a little before 2:00 a.m.

God, Roland might as well have been here and shaken him awake! Lucan's heart was beating too quickly, but he resumed his position under the covers, backing up against Court. He should make Court go, but the bed was so warm with him here.

"Who's Ro?" Court asked. His sleepy voice was the sexiest thing ever, and his hand running up and down Lucan's arm was far more comforting than it should have been.

"One of my roommates. Everybody hates me tonight. It's fine."

"I don't hate you." Court's voice rumbled against Lucan's ear. When Court kissed his shoulder, his stubble scraped tantalizingly against Lucan's skin, and then Court rubbed Lucan's chest, stomach, hip.

The sensations kept Lucan's heart rate up; he wished they didn't feel so good. Court hooked his strong, furred leg over Lucan and pressed his pelvis against Lucan's lower back. An unmistakable hardness poked at the base of Lucan's spine, and Court rubbed it there, rubbed, rubbed—

"Stop." Lucan was in a different headspace now—not as desperately submissive as he'd been earlier tonight, even if his voice came out breathy and unconvincing.

"Why?" asked Court, defensive.

The tone made Lucan's resolve harder. "You said you wanted me to teach you."

"Yeah, but—" Court didn't finish the sentence as he palmed Lucan's dick through his boxers.

Lucan grappled at Court's wrist, scratching him.

"Ow!"

"Ask me." Power buzzed in Lucan's skin—a new sensation, vengeful, a little wrong. "Ask me like a good boy."

Court growled, and the animalistic sound touched Lucan somewhere deep. In a second, he was face-first in his pillow with Court's cock, encased in the soft fabric of his underwear, sliding slow and hard against the crack of Lucan's ass. "I'm no one's boy."

Lucan's skin burned with a shameful kind of pleasure, but there was fear there, too. Was Court not going to listen to him?

But fuck that. Lucan knew what Court liked, and he wouldn't let him have it if he didn't cooperate. They were going to do things *right* this time.

"Ask me, Court. Say, 'May I fuck you?' Or I'm done. I won't get into this. Whatever you do, I'll just lie here. I don't give a fuck."

Court gripped Lucan's hair, nails scraping his scalp. The grip was rough, but it made Lucan break out in goose bumps and tingles. He clenched his hole involuntarily, imagining Court's cock forcing its way in.

Court turned Lucan's head to the side and whispered into his ear. "May I fuck you?" He didn't move anymore, didn't hump Lucan's ass, though he remained pressed tightly against him.

Lucan arched his back and breathed through his mouth. "Yes." His anger disappeared with his resolve. There was more to the things they liked to do: limits, safewords. But Lucan's lizard brain was satisfied for now, and he sunk into the mattress, gave himself up.

"Oh, babe." Court's voice was heavy with adoration. "I love you like this." His nails scraped Lucan's hips as he found the band of his boxers and yanked the fabric away.

Soon, bare cock and rough pubic hair met Lucan's backside, and he reached mindlessly for the nightstand drawer, fingers catching on the metal pull. He groped for a condom and lube but found neither.

Wishful thinking—it had been too long since he'd had a guy in his room to have supplies at the ready. There were some under the bed, tucked into a box with his lube and his toys for the frequent times he got off alone. But Court didn't need to see all that, and he'd manage to look, especially if Lucan tried to be secretive about it. Lucan could just imagine Court going through everything, wanting to use it all at once, persuading Lucan to go too far and too hard for one night.

They weren't ready for that; they might not ever be. What if this was just long-overdue breakup sex—a way for them to get closure?

Lucan whined, head swirling, cock softening. He always tried so hard to keep it together, but he was too emotional, and he crumbled at the most inconvenient times.

"Hey." Gently, Court turned Lucan onto his back. "What's wrong?"

"I'm not prepared. I didn't think this would happen." *You should just go.*

Towering above Lucan, Court was so confident and easy, his short bangs messy against his forehead. "You thought you could be around me for more than two minutes and not give it up?"

"Yeah."

Court smirked fondly. "Stupid." He hovered over Lucan, staring into his eyes.

Lucan couldn't look away even though he wanted to. It had been a long time since he'd been with someone like this—in bed, staring, naked. It had been different in the car.

Court got closer, falling like an asteroid about to hit Earth—

Lucan turned his head, and Court's lips collided with his cheek. Lucan both felt and heard him sigh.

"So I can't kiss you?" Court's whole body covered Lucan's. He found Lucan's hands and pinned them against the sheets. "I can fuck you, but I can't kiss you? You're upset; I'm trying to make it better."

Lucan clamped his eyes shut, but that only intensified the sensations that came with Court's weight on him: their cocks mushed together, their skin touching at countless contact points, Court's mouth against Lucan's neck. Then there was Court saying these things that he'd never said before. *I'm trying to make it better.*

Lucan ignored how good this felt, how right despite everything. "You have to ask first."

"Do I have to ask for everything?"

"No, but..." The urge to give in burned at the edges of Lucan's brain, but he forced himself to focus on protocol. "We haven't negotiated. We haven't talked about limits or safewords or anything. I can't just let you do whatever you want."

Court scoffed. "I wasn't planning on spanking you anymore tonight. Or doing anything else we used to do. So we don't need that shit."

"That's not really how it works."

"You're the expert." Court's tone held a bite of sarcasm, and in the lamplight, his gaze was fierce, black. "May I kiss you?"

As twisted up as he was inside, Lucan's lips tingled in anticipation. He loved kissing. When he'd first joined the BDSM scene, he'd been free with his lips and tongue. He'd made out with Dom once in a bar bathroom at a slosh, and a few times, when he was feeling particularly submissive, he'd let a couple of Femdoms have at him, too. Kissing Court had always been something he'd done in the throes of subspace, not as foreplay or whatever this was, but he'd been shyer back then, and Court had been far more focused on getting high and getting off.

"Yes," Lucan said.

Court rolled them onto their sides. He held Lucan's face and gave him several small, slow pecks. Funny how he did warm-up here and not with spanking, but it gave Lucan a chance to get into it, to relax.

As the kissing grew deeper, Lucan let his hand trail down Court's hard back and settle on one sculpted ass cheek. When they'd dated before, Court had had muscle, but not like this. This was a porn-star-level body, and Lucan had never been touched by someone like that. He might feel self-conscious about his own underdeveloped muscles if Court wasn't so obviously attracted to him.

Court licked into Lucan's mouth, and Lucan moaned, continuing to palm and knead at Court's ass. He didn't Top—in the BDSM way or otherwise—very often, but he wondered what it would be like to have Court that way, to see him vulnerable for once and breaking apart with internal pleasure.

Court took Lucan's lip between his teeth and bit hard enough to make him whimper.

When he let go, he rested his forehead on Lucan's. "I learned the term for what you are."

"Hmm?"

"Pain slut."

Lucan rolled his eyes. "I don't know about that."

"Oh yeah? Which do you like better?" Court stroked gently down Lucan's side. On a second pass, he scratched down the same stretch of skin. The first touch did mostly nothing for Lucan, but the second made him press closer to Court, seeking more sensation. The reaction was involuntary.

Court laughed. "See?"

"Dom doesn't hurt me, and I play with him all the time."

"Do you get subby or whatever?"

"Yeah." But there were versions of subspace. One kind made Lucan relax and drift, and it was nice. But the other sent blood spilling into his groin, made him pant and moan uncontrollably, broke time, made everything solid disappear. Pain and psychological submission could do the latter, but Dom's gentle feathers, thuddy floggers, and soft-core metal toys could not. Though the knives he'd used the other night had come close.

Still, Lucan preferred the safety of a calmer high. He hardly ever experienced sub drop with Dom, and any marks he got were superficial and didn't last long enough for him to regret them. How he felt with Court, on the other hand, was dangerous. When one's mental defenses were down, they couldn't speak up for themselves, couldn't make sure they weren't doing long-term damage for one night of good sex or a temporary flood of endorphins.

"On your FetNet profile, it says masochist," said Court.

Damn it; he needed to set his profile to Private. "What are you getting at?"

"I'm saying I can give you what you need." Court's big hand slid down Lucan's spine and brushed between his ass cheeks, just barely grazing his hole. "Do you remember the day I used my belt on you?"

It was a memory Lucan only brought out when no other fantasy could get him there. "Yeah." Even now, he remembered clearly the way he'd felt—sick, scared, humiliated, unbelievably hard and wanting. He'd shown up at Court's apartment fifteen minutes later than he'd promised, and Court hadn't said anything when he'd opened the door. He'd just yanked Lucan inside, bent him over the arm of the couch, and pulled down his pants. Lucan had expected to be fucked, but instead, Court had slipped his belt out of his jeans and looped it, ready to swat.

"When I say 1:00, do I mean 1:15?" he'd asked.

Lucan had been too stunned to reply.

"Answer me! When I say 1:00, do I mean 1:15?"

"N-No."

"That's right. And I'm going to make sure you never show up late again."

Court had started the hits then. Lucan remembered staring out the window at the stark sunlight, so normal and everyday compared to this thing that was happening. He'd been so into it that he'd leaked precum onto the couch, and though Court had fucked him—bareback, always —he hadn't come inside him. Instead, he'd come all over Lucan's welted ass.

In the present, Lucan burned. He was fully hard now, and so was Court. Reluctantly, he pulled away from Court's alluring body, but only to get on the floor and find his toy box.

From the bed, Court asked, "What are you doing?"

"Getting you a condom."

Court groaned. "Oh, come on."

Thud, thud, click; Lucan undid the latches on his hefty box full of kinky goodies. After lifting the lid, he rifled through the disorganized leather, metal, and silicone until he found the little bottle of lube and the condoms he put over his dildo whenever he fucked himself.

Court's gaze was heavy on him. "Is that your BDSM stuff?"

"Yep."

Court hung off the bed, reaching. "Let me—"

"No." Lucan slammed the box shut and shoved it back under the bed. He tossed the condom and lube to Court.

Court squinted. "I got tested like two months ago. We just need this." He held up the lube.

"Yeah, that's not good enough. Condom or no penetration."

"I love it when you talk dirty."

Lucan ignored the immature jibe as he rejoined Court on the bed. Nerves fluttering in his stomach, he lay down on his back.

"Turn over," said Court.

"No."

"Aw." Court's eyes twinkled mischievously. "You want to stare deeply into my eyes while I *penetrate* you?"

"No. I just want to make sure you actually wear that condom." And that he didn't slip it off when Lucan couldn't see or was too wrapped up in sensation to notice.

The light went out of Court's eyes. "Have a little faith."

Lucan wished he could. But it wasn't just that Court had hurt him. Lucan had trouble trusting any Dominant these days. He'd met too many who were so focused on getting their rocks off that they threw protocol out the window. Some of them did it proudly; they purposefully went after novice subs.

Court wasn't like *that*. But he was forceful and brash, and a few words spoken in the right tone made Lucan want to throw protocol out, too, like he had just a few hours ago when he'd let Court have his way in the car.

He couldn't let that happen again. He had to stay alert.

"I wish you'd relax." Court was only half-hard, and he stroked himself, presumably in an effort to get his cock ready for the condom. "I can feel you not relaxing, and it's stressing me out. It's like you don't want this."

This was the one thing Lucan had to his advantage: Court got off on his sub getting off, too.

Lucan consciously relaxed his body, hooking his hands over the headboard and spreading his legs. "I want it." His chest clenched when he thought of what to say next. Part of him didn't want to share, but he had no doubt it would make Court feel better. "I still think about the stuff you did to me sometimes. When I'm fucking myself with my dildo."

Court gave Lucan a heated look. "Don't bullshit me."

"I wish I was lying."

Court's cock got fully hard again, jutting out from his stomach as he fiddled with the condom, but Lucan wanted even more of a reaction.

"The night I first saw you again, Dom used knives on me, and I had a flashback to that time you cut me in the kitchen." Lucan's groin heated and throbbed, and his cheeks burned in protest to the vulnerable words he was spilling. "Before I cuddled with Dom, I jacked off in the bathroom thinking about you pounding me against the fridge."

Court had the condom on now, and he stared at Lucan intensely. "You don't need to fantasize anymore. Hold your legs back."

Lucan obeyed, and he clenched his hole in anticipation of being stretched and filled.

Court drizzled lube between Lucan's cheeks and rubbed the smooth, rubber-encased head of his cock in it—back and forth, back and forth, teasing, prepping.

"Just shove it in." Lucan didn't care if it hurt. He kind of wanted it to, but he fucked himself so much with toys that it shouldn't do more than ache a bit at first.

Court's gaze snapped up to meet Lucan's. "I'll fuck you how I see fit."

"Yes, Sir." The words just came out, and Lucan's cheeks heated in embarrassment.

Court's full mouth tilted in an arrogant smirk. "Good boy."

Ugh. Lucan loved that so much; he was so typical!

His frustration with himself must have shown in his face because Court chuckled and leaned down to peck Lucan on the cheek. "You're so cute." Then he shoved his cock in all at once just how Lucan had asked.

The stretch was delicious—fuller, softer, more *right* than any silicone cock or stainless steel plug. It did ache a little, but Lucan lapped up the sensation like a hot, thirsty dog at a cold bowl of water.

"Is this what you like?" Court pulled almost all the way out before slamming back home again.

"Yes," Lucan hissed and wrapped his legs around Court's sculpted torso. *Protocol, protocol...* "May I scratch you?" Lucan had scratched Court's biceps in the car, but the red lines weren't there anymore, just like the tenderness on Lucan's ass cheeks had all but disappeared.

"Do your worst." Court rutted his hips, and Lucan blinked slowly, trying to keep his eyes open and his mind more than a mess of endorphins.

"Thank you." He didn't mean to moan the words, but his gratitude was as thick as Court's cock rubbing at his sweet spot. This was perfect, and the rhythm Court was setting had Lucan's anxiety falling away, bringing forth that lizard brain that only cared about pleasure.

"You feel so good," Court whispered, and Lucan couldn't answer with words, only groans and his own erratic rutting intensifying their fusion.

Some guys didn't like all the work involved with bottoming for anal. You had to be clean and stretched and lubed-up, but Lucan lived for it. There was nothing better than a man wrapped around him, in him, taking over all his senses. He'd been living on disembodied plastic for far too long.

The condom was necessary, but he wished he could hold Court's spend and feel it ooze out of him afterward. He wanted a sore hole from a hard fucking, and that he could get either way.

"Harder!" He tapped Court with his foot.

"I'm not a damn horse." Court folded over Lucan and pressed a damp forehead to his temple. "You're just a slut for it, aren't you? Like a bitch in heat 24/7. I know you're—"

Lucan dug his nails into Court's back so hard his top knuckles ached.

Court growled that irresistible, primal growl. "You asked for it." And he set a rough pace, sending the bed rocking with each thrust, his pelvis snapping against Lucan's ass.

Lucan writhed for the dick, hungry for the pounding. "Yes," he moaned. "Yes, Court." He made a pitiful sound each time Court's cock slid home. He was so full, his skin becoming raw from the relentless friction. He only wished he could have more pain. He should have let Court get in his toy box, pull out some nipple clamps or something.

"Hurt me." Lucan needed it, just one bite of pain somewhere to supplement the pleasure. His cock was rock hard, his whole groin full of blood, but he needed more, just a little more. "Please, Court."

Court slowed his punishing thrusts. He was breathing hard, and when Lucan petted his back, the skin was damp.

"You're a workout," he breathed. "My abs are burning."

"Hurt me," Lucan repeated. "I'm a pain slut. You're right."

Court swept his hands up Lucan's sides and stopped with his thumbnails pressed into Lucan's nipples.

It was a nice tease, but it still wasn't enough.

"More." How could he explain? There was a level of pain that would make everything perfect, but he wouldn't know until he got it.

Court pinched Lucan's nipples and twisted. He snapped his hips, thrusting deep, and that was it—Lucan cried out as his balls emptied and he shot between them.

Court pulled out.

"Did you come?" Lucan asked, dazed, voice heavy.

He got his answer when Court pulled off the condom and stroked himself. "Show me your hole."

It took all of Lucan's post-orgasm strength to hold his legs back, presenting his well-used hole. *Oh, fuck. He's going to come on me, he's going to—*

Court yelled as his dick shot and spurts of cum landed on Lucan's tender opening.

The filthy sensation made Lucan clench, his stomach tumbling. "Court..."

Court flopped down onto his back. "You wear me out. Talk in the morning." He groped for Lucan's side and patted him gently with a moist hand. "Promise."

Lucan slowly lowered his legs and, with some tissues from a box on the nightstand, wiped himself clean. Then he shut off the lamp.

Court's steady breathing and lack of response when Lucan curled up to him signified he'd already passed out, and it left Lucan a little cold. But he snuggled up tightly to the sweat-damp form and pulled the top sheet over them both. Luckily, it took only a few more minutes for him to join Court in sleep.

CHAPTER 7

COURT DIDN'T WANT to move from this spot. He had to piss, but Lucan was sleeping so soundly against his side, and he was sure when he moved, Lucan would immediately wake up and tell Court all the stuff he'd done wrong last night, whatever he'd done.

Court wasn't usually so negative, but he'd been lying here for at least an hour thinking about the past: how Lucan was right about him ignoring texts, but he hadn't said a single thing about it back then. Court wouldn't answer some innocent text like "Hey, how are you?" and the next time they'd see each other, Lucan would act like everything was fine. He remembered Lucan being moody a lot, but he'd always gotten into a better mood after they had sex.

Lucan stirred, and Court froze, doing his best to keep the peaceful moment, but Lucan was pushing himself up and opening his eyes.

"Hey," he said and smiled.

"Hey."

Lucan's smile disappeared. "What's wrong?"

"Nothing. I need to pee."

"Okay."

Court headed for the door, his morning wood on full display.

"Wait!" Lucan lunged for a closet and pulled out a blue robe before tossing it to Court. "I have roommates."

"Right." The robe was tight, but he managed to keep it closed and not rip the seams as he made his way to the bathroom and back again. In the bedroom, Lucan was sitting cross-legged on the unmade bed in his boxers, chewing on a nail.

He stopped chewing. "So are we going to talk?"

Court vaguely remembered telling Lucan they would before he'd passed out last night. "Sure." For some reason, it felt like the bars of a cage were about to come down on him.

"You better tell me what's wrong," said Lucan. "Or did you just wake up grumpy?"

"I'm waiting for the laundry list."

Lucan creased his brow, apparently confused.

"Oh, you know." Court sat down on the edge of the bed, the robe pulling taut over his shoulders. "How I fucked up last night even though you shot like a rocket?"

Lucan's cheeks pinked beautifully in the streaks of sunlight coming from the window. "Last night was fine."

Court scoffed. "Fine?" It had been more than fine; it had been fucking fire! Court hadn't even minded the condom, especially since he'd still gotten to come on Lucan's beautiful ass.

"There are some things we'd need to work on if..." Lucan averted his eyes, played with his bangs that honestly needed washed.

Court probably looked like a greasy mess himself after all the sweating they'd done together. Would Lucan shower with him?

"Court?" Lucan peered at Court shyly.

"What?"

"What do you want to happen with us?"

Court stiffened against a pain in his chest. How could Lucan ask that? "You know what I want."

"Not really."

"I want you. It's pretty damn simple."

"Nothing's simple." Lucan fiddled with the little black ring in his septum. "This could be the end of it. Great sex, closure—"

"Fuck you."

"I'm just saying!"

Anger blazed a path through Court's whole body, and he lunged, pulling Lucan into a rough kiss. He didn't care if they were dirty, if they hadn't brushed their teeth. Lucan was his, and he would stay his. It felt too right. It just made sense. This was not ending.

He bit into Lucan's lip before he pulled away, and Lucan touched the spot gingerly.

"There's no closure," said Court.

Lucan winced. "You're right."

"What do you want me to say?"

"Just what you want. Specifically. I want to know that before I tell you what my conditions are."

"What are your conditions?"

Lucan scoffed softly. "Ideally, am I your submissive? Your FetNet profile says, 'just in the bedroom' so—"

"Yeah. I don't want someone crawling after me in puppy ears or some shit 24/7."

Lucan laughed, a single syllable of sound before he stopped himself. "I'm not into puppy play."

"You know what I mean."

"I think so, yeah." Lucan played with the edge of a mussed sheet, and Court sensed he was stalling what he wanted to say.

"Just spit it out," said Court.

"You have to let me teach you. You have to do everything I say when it comes to consent and limits. We have to really negotiate stuff before we do any type of sex again or play or anything."

Court's instinct was to get defensive. It was like Lucan was telling him he had to do a mound of paperwork every time he wanted to nut. But he knew he'd say yes if it would keep Lucan from saying stupid things like "This could be the end of it."

"Okay," he said.

Lucan looked into Court's eyes like he was trying to see if he was serious.

"I'm not bullshitting you," said Court. "I'll do what you want."

"Okay." Lucan ran a hand down Court's arm as if to comfort him. "After a while, it's not as big of a deal. Some of the stuff becomes second nature. After we decide some stuff, we don't have to talk about it again unless we want to change it or clarify."

Court didn't really know what that meant, but he nodded. "Okay."

Lucan took Court's hand and played gently with his fingers. "We don't have to get really in-depth with it right now, but if we're going to be something again, I'm monogamous. You can't Top anyone else."

Court wanted to scream. "I think that goes without saying."

"Not r—"

"Yes, it does! And you better not pull any of that crap where you act like you want to fuck someone else to get a reaction out of me."

Lucan looked away guiltily, and Court resisted the urge to dredge up any more of the past, at least for right now.

"I should get going," said Court. He had work at 3:00. "What time is it?" His phone was in his pants but probably dead.

Lucan checked his phone. "Twelve thirty." He turned over Court's hand and walked his fingers across his palm. "Do you have time to shower with me?" The way he asked it, with his pale eyes all big and pleading, made Court's cock give a twitch of interest. God, he hoped none of Lucan's roommates had taken over the shower since he'd pissed.

"Yeah, I can make that work."

Lucan grinned and hopped up. "No sex, though. We still haven't negotiated properly, and—"

"Yeah, yeah." Court gave Lucan a light swat on the butt, and Lucan rolled his eyes in a long-suffering manner, as if the years they'd been apart had never happened. Court sent up a silent prayer to the BDSM gods: *Let me keep him this time.*

* * *

Lucan's insides were a jumble, like there was a little tornado spinning, spinning, spinning inside him. On the porch under the shade of the awning, Court gave him a minty goodbye kiss with tongue that made Lucan feel even hotter in the dry summer heat.

"Don't get mad after I leave," he said near Lucan's lips.

"What?" Lucan asked.

"You know..." Court gestured vaguely as if he was having trouble coming up with the words. "Don't decide this was shit when it wasn't."

Lucan didn't think he'd ever seen Court's eyes like this—unsure, scared. It made the tornado inside him move faster. He realized when he'd let things slide that he'd also thrown out the specific talking that came with aftercare: discussing how things went, what they'd liked and hadn't liked, reassuring each other that they weren't harboring secret, negative feelings.

"First lesson." He took Court's hands in his. "Usually, after a scene, we talk about how it went. I tell you if I liked everything or not, and you tell me."

Court licked his lips. "Okay."

Lucan glanced around to make sure none of his neighbors were in earshot. They weren't, but Lucan still spoke against Court's ear. "I liked when you came on my ass."

Court gripped the back of Lucan's shirt.

"But—" Lucan pulled back enough to point at Court's face. "We can't do anything else like that until we both get tested. It's too risky."

Court's eyes were lit up with satisfied mischief. "All right."

"Now tell me something you liked."

"All of it."

Lucan chuckled. "Something specific."

"Okay." Court's gaze got distant for a second. "I liked when you surrendered. After you made me ask if I could fuck you, and you said yes. I love that." Court pulled Lucan flush against him. "Love when you go soft."

Court kissed Lucan's ear, and over Court's shoulder, Lucan spotted Mr. Abner across the street coming out his front door.

He pushed Court away as gently as he could. "Yeah, so normally we would talk about it for longer than this, but you said you have work." Lucan had work, too.

"Yeah." Court gave Lucan another searing kiss, and Lucan forgot about Mr. Abner. When they pulled apart, he caught the old man staring from his mailbox.

"Bye." Lucan retreated toward the door.

"Bye, babe." Court's smile dazzled before he got into the car he'd pushed Lucan against just hours ago. If anyone had told Lucan when he'd arrived at last night's party that he'd be here the next morning, watching Court go with a tentative happiness in his veins, he'd have slapped them.

But as soon as he went back into the house, reality set in. Dom was sitting on the couch with his phone, and he glanced up with a stony expression.

Lucan wanted badly to ignore him. It was almost 2:00 now, he had to be at the restaurant at 4:00, and he still needed to eat breakfast. But Dom was his best friend, and he couldn't have animosity between them. Plus, they'd have to talk about the fact that Court would be taking up Lucan's playtime. They'd agreed Court wouldn't Top anyone else, which meant Lucan couldn't bottom for Dom anymore.

Lucan sat down on the couch next to him.

Dom was playing some kind of game with arcade-like sound effects. After a few tense seconds of Lucan waiting in silence, Dom set his phone aside.

"Fun night?" he asked.

Yeah, aside from the parts where you and Ro were yelling at me. "You could say that."

"Guess you changed your mind about Court." Dom smirked cruelly. "Was it the six-pack abs that did it?"

Lucan squinted. "*You* have a six pack."

Dom's abs were covered, but he still pulled at his T-shirt as if to make sure they really were.

"Come on," said Lucan. "You know me. I wouldn't take off with someone just because they're hot." But this crap about Court wasn't important. He needed to apologize—again. Rip off the Band-Aid, show Dom his underbelly. He'd been an asshole last night even if he felt incapable of doing anything except what he'd done. "I'm sorry. I should have thought about you and our plans. Court pulled me away to talk, and he pushed me against the car, and I just..." Lucan didn't want to overshare, but Dom was watching him expectantly. "I love how he makes me feel, and I lost my head and hurt your feelings. Then after we fought, I felt like shit, so I had Court take me home. I should have let you, Roland, or Erin know that he'd given me a ride."

"You *should* have told him you'd meet up with him after we scened. That would have been the respectful thing to do."

Lucan winced. "You're right."

"I figured you'd gone with him. You're an adult. That part's whatever."

"Okay."

Dom sighed through his nose. Then he picked up his phone and went back to his game. "Thanks for apologizing."

Lucan could tell he'd been dismissed. He needed to tell Dom the rest, about his plans with Court and how they'd affect their arrangement. He also just wanted to tell him because he was excited about it, and Dom was who he told stuff to, but now wasn't the time.

He headed for the kitchen. Of course, Roland was in there pouring himself a bowl of cereal. Chest tight, Lucan went for his box of granola bars and hid behind the cabinet door.

"So when's the collaring ceremony?" Roland asked.

Lucan closed the cabinet.

Roland wiggled his eyebrows, and Lucan grinned, relieved that Roland had apparently gotten over his anger in a matter of hours like always. Lucan should have had faith, but he'd worried Dom being pissed at him as well would have given Roland's negative feelings staying power.

"There's no collaring ceremony." Lucan tore open the wrapper on his breakfast. "We just made an arrangement."

"Oh yeah?" Roland took a bite of his bran.

"Yeah. Court doesn't know what goes into safe, sane, and consensual kink, so I'm going to teach him."

"Mhm."

"Yeah, I know. Sounds good in theory, right?"

Roland pointed with his spoon. "You said it. Good luck, though, man."

"Thanks." Lucan tore into his granola bar. As he chewed, he made his way to his bedroom closet. He had a shirt clean for work but apparently no pants.

"Dammit," he muttered. Stupid uniform. It wasn't like the button-up and trousers were any help where tips were concerned, but the owners of the restaurant where he worked wanted the place to feel classier than it was. The main thing served was pizza, and there were a million pizzerias in Pittsburgh.

Begrudgingly, Lucan got his dirty clothes together and, at the last second, pulled the sheets from his bed as well. The memory of digging his nails into Court's back resurfaced, then the one of being penetrated, and he had to take a second to compose himself. He didn't have time to jack off, and he didn't need the inconvenience of a hard-on. Still, once he'd calmed down, he couldn't help thinking of some of the things he wanted to do with Court in the context of their new arrangement. Bondage, impact, knives... The options were infinite.

CHAPTER 8

COURT HAD MADE it home with just enough time to get his uniform, wave to Cally where she sat at her computer, and get to work. It was a slow night, starting off with an alcoholism call (the kid would be fine) but then nothing for a few hours.

That was probably for the best. Court was distracted. His head was full of last night, of Lucan's skin, eyes, lips, ass, words whispered against Court's ear. He hadn't wanted to leave this afternoon. Not when Lucan was being soft to him instead of prickly like he'd been at first. He was willing to kiss Court, willing to be touched, ready for Court to take him over. Court was itching to get back to him, whenever that would be.

Two more calls and the work night was over, and Court hadn't expended enough energy. He checked his phone, hoping for a text, but there weren't any. He sent one to Lucan: *When do I get to see you again?* But Lucan didn't answer right away.

At home, Court found Cally curled up on the sofa watching *The Walking Dead*. Now that her workday was over—she worked from home doing something internet-y—she paused the show and turned her attention toward Court.

"You met someone." Her face, which looked like Court's but rounder, held a warm, excited expression.

Court couldn't help but smile back. "'Met' isn't the word."

"Cryptic."

"Do you remember that boyfriend I had in college?" As soon as he'd said it, it felt wrong. *That boyfriend*—like Lucan was just one boyfriend of many and not the only one who'd left a meaningful impression.

"I remember Lucan," said Cally, and the light had left her eyes. "How could I forget the guy you dropped out of school over?"

Court should have known he'd get this kind of reaction out of Cally. She'd been there for him when it had all gone down, answering his unhinged phone calls and emotional texts at 3:00 a.m.

Still, the negativity put a damper on his joy. "I don't regret dropping out of school. I like my job."

"Yeah, but that's not the point."

"I get where you're coming from. But it's the breakup that was the problem, not Lucan." Court leaned on the back of the sofa. "We never should have broken up in the first place." Court's insides tried to get stormy thinking like that, but he swallowed the anger. He didn't want to resent Lucan for dumping him back then. He wanted to feel like he'd felt on Lucan's porch, like there were helium-filled balloons under his feet, pushing him high, high, high.

"All I care about is that you're happy, and that whoever you're with treats you well." Cally smiled, but Court was her twin; he knew it was fake as shit.

Court shrugged. "So far, so good."

Cally unpaused her show, filling the living room with zombie screeches, and Court headed to the kitchen to get a smartwater. When he checked his phone, there was a text from Lucan waiting.

Sorry, I was taking a bath. We can meet up soon, but I have to get prepared first

Prepared how? Court drank his water and wished it were a beer, but he'd given up alcohol a few years ago to help trim any unnecessary calories in his diet. He usually worked out in the mornings, but he'd skipped the gym today on account of having Lucan in his arms. Maybe they could work out together sometime? Court had tried to get Cally to go with him several times, but she didn't like exercise.

If I'm going to teach you, I need to have lesson plans, don't I?

Court grimaced at the idea of lesson plans. *Didn't realize this was going to be so formal.* He went into his bedroom to get ready for bed, though it was mostly out of habit; he wasn't tired at all.

It needs to be a little formal or I'll lose my cool and not do things right

Don't you want to lose your cool? Wasn't that the whole point? Court hadn't been in the fetish community for very long, but it seemed to him that the whole thing was built around losing yourself in another person.

Not yet. You have to earn it

Lucan's words did bad things to Court's stomach. He stripped out of his uniform, put on pajama pants, brushed his teeth. By then, he was annoyed enough to send a reckless text. But wasn't he the Dominant?

I don't like being talked to like a bad sub, Lucan.

I don't know how else to word it

Try harder.

Fine. I need to feel safer before I let go completely. Is that better, Sir?

Hot satisfaction replaced Court's anger. He wished Lucan were here so he could channel it into a reddened ass. But he wouldn't put Lucan through another spanking so soon. Maybe something else.

Teach me. What kind of punishments are there besides spanking? I think you deserve something.

We haven't talked about if we want to do discipline stuff

I do. Didn't you like it when I used to punish you? After Lucan had dumped him, Court had tried not to think about those times; the mix of arousal and hurt had been too much for him to handle. But with Lucan in his grasp again, he'd been letting the memories surface. Now, he recalled the time Lucan had failed a test and come to Court crying and begging to be punished for the bad grade. At first, Court had felt strange about it, what with Lucan teary-eyed already. But the spanking he'd given him that night had been one of the most satisfying. Lucan had been so open to him, raw.

Yes, Sir. We should talk about Sir too. Do you like being called that?

You know I do.

There are other options

Like?

Master (but I don't like this one), Boss, Lord, Alpha, Captain, Dom (but I know a Dom, so let's not), Wolf, King, Sire (meh), Commander, others I can't think of right now

Court couldn't help but chuckle at some of the suggestions. Sir was nice. But Alpha, Wolf, and King appealed to him as well.

I'm not sure. Can we try them?

Yes. What do I call you right now?

Let's try King.

Yes, King.

Eh, Court didn't know about that one.

Lucan sent a link, and it led to a blog post with the title "50+ Punishment Ideas for Your BDSM Relationship." *Don't get set on any until we talk about limits, please.*

The post had everything. Punishments included writing lines (the example given: *I do not come without permission* 100 times), being denied attention, cock and ball torture, being forced to wear a vibrator in public, naked cleaning, caning... The list went on and on.

Wow, Court texted.

Overwhelmed? ;)

A little.

I only like some.

This post says you're not supposed to like it.

Where's the pouting emoji?

Court found himself grinning. He didn't want to punish Lucan. He wanted to kiss him, pull him close, see him smile and laugh.

When do I get to see you again? He knew he was being pushy asking another time, but he couldn't help it. He'd be around Lucan 24/7 if he could.

Soon. I'll let you know in a couple days when I'm free

You'd better, or I really will have to punish you.

* * *

Lucan was having trouble getting out of the bathtub. In the whirlwind of his new arrangement with Court, he'd actually forgotten about the threat of sub drop, and now he was sitting under the lukewarm spray from the showerhead, crying for no other explicable reason.

It was amazing what endorphins could do. Lucan had been in such a good mood the last couple of days that he'd stupidly thought it was because things were going well. He'd had sex with Court—twice—and nothing bad had happened. He'd convinced Court to listen to him, and Court had agreed to shape up for him. Lucan had gotten to do the kind of play he liked, and he was going to get to do even more of it in the future. Court was even answering texts!

Now, naked and wet with a sinking hole in his chest, Lucan knew all of that was head-in-the-clouds bullshit. Or at least, he'd been way happier than he should have been. So what if Court had followed Lucan's guidance so far? It didn't mean shit. Lucan hadn't even made him do things all-the-way right. And anyway, Court just wanted another fuck!

A different part of Lucan's brain whispered that this was the drop talking. And he buried his head in his arms and blubbered into the quickly cooling shower water.

He thought of Dom and the safe scene they could have had together if Lucan hadn't been so weak to Court's advances that night. Dom was right about how Lucan had treated him. He'd acted like a frenzied sub and put the promise of pleasure over his best fucking friend, and that was not okay. Nothing about any of this was okay.

How had Lucan gotten back here? After all these years, how was he a crying mess for Court *again*?

When the water got too cold to bear, Lucan finally shut it off. Without the white noise of the water hitting the shower's surfaces, another sound was audible: Lucan's phone was ringing.

Getting shakily to his feet, Lucan got out of the tub and checked his phone with a wet hand.

Court!

He swiped to answer, grabbed a towel, wiped his hands and the phone. When he got the phone to his ear finally, Court was saying "Hello? Hello?"

"Court! Sorry, uh—"

"You should be sorry. You said you'd text me, and now you're, what—avoiding me?"

Lucan froze at the roughness in Court's voice. It touched him in his aching places, and he wasn't sure if he liked it or not.

"You got all over my dick about not answering texts when we were together, but now you're not answering mine. I mean, if you were working or something, I get it... Shit, I just feel awful about things. I want to see you. Do you not want to see me? Luc."

In the face of Court's rambling desperation, Lucan's mind grew clearer. Fuck, they were *both* dropping, weren't they? And maybe the thoughts that had had Lucan sobbing in the bath were warranted (and maybe not), but regardless, Lucan had promised to teach Court. He needed to teach about this, too.

"I do want to see you," he said. "When are you free?"

"Now. Are you busy today?"

Lucan didn't have to go to the restaurant, but he did have other work. Freelance stuff with deadlines. If he busted his ass tomorrow, though, he could put it off for today.

"No," he said.

"I'm coming over."

"Okay."

"See you soon." Court didn't say goodbye before hanging up.

After he dried his hair, Lucan caught a glimpse of himself in the bathroom mirror. His puffy, red eyes would be a dead giveaway to Court that he'd been crying.

Oh, well. Maybe seeing Lucan like this would make sub drop more real for Court. And there was the fact that Lucan had used to fantasize about Court catching him when he was upset. Court would be his emotional white knight and tend valiantly to his psychological wounds. Instead, Lucan had failed to show Court his pain and communicate that he needed comforting.

Lucan wouldn't make the same mistake this time. He'd take what he needed with both hands and make sure Court's eyes were open when he did it.

* * *

About twenty minutes later, Court was pounding on Lucan's front door. The only other person in the house was Erin, and she focused big eyes on Lucan as he raced through the living room toward the thudding.

"It's okay." Lucan glanced at the textbook in Erin's lap. "We'll just be in my room."

"*Oh*," Erin answered suggestively.

Lucan flung open the door.

Immediately, Court was on him, touching his face, looking at his stupid, tear-damaged eyes. "Baby, you've been—"

"Shh. Let's go to my room. Come on." Lucan took Court's hand and led him away from Erin's prying eyes and up the stairs.

As soon as they'd crossed the threshold into Lucan's bedroom, Court pressed him to the nearest wall. It was lucky Lucan didn't have a lot of decor hanging.

"You've been crying," Court whispered.

The words and intense look Court gave him made Lucan's stomach tumble, his heart race. He both loved and hated being this vulnerable, being forced open to Court's gaze. Court was in his skin, and he apparently gave a shit that he was in there, and Lucan wanted sex. Oh, God, he wanted sex.

He was messed up. No—he was *kinky*.

"Crying over me?" Court asked.

Lucan nodded; he didn't trust himself to speak.

"And you weren't going to tell me, were you? Instead, you ignored me."

It was true; Court had sent Lucan three texts before he'd called. Lucan hadn't ignored them, though. He hadn't even seen them. He'd been too wrapped up in his own emotional tailspin.

"I'm sorry," he whispered.

"I'm not the bad guy for once, huh?"

"Right, King."

Court held Lucan's face and wiped his thumb down his lips. "Call me Alpha today."

"Yes, Alpha." That was *so* much better than King. Lucan pulled away from the wall to hide against Court's warm chest. "My Alpha." He gripped the front of Court's T-shirt, scratching the muscles underneath. This was a familiar place, heady. He whined a little and nuzzled against the soft fabric.

It had been too long, too long...

Court slid his hand, heavy and protective, down Lucan's spine. "There's something I'd like you to wear for me."

Anxiety put a crack in Lucan's contentment. "I can't have the talk with you right now. I'm—I'm having sub drop."

"What talk?" Court reached into his pocket, and whatever he was retrieving clinked together—metal. He brought out a pair of nipple clamps.

Lucan gingerly inspected them in Court's palm. They were adjustable, so they didn't have to be too harsh. But they could be, which was what Lucan preferred.

"The talk about what's allowed and what's not," he said. "Limits, safety." At the moment, it sounded tedious, but Lucan could never admit that. Safety was important. He'd dug up some index cards so they could write out their limits. Then again, nipple clamps weren't one of his.

"Yeah, but I researched these. They're the safest kind, and I'll make sure we don't keep them on for longer than ten minutes."

"I can do twenty."

"Okay then. Pull up your shirt."

Panic threatened to flare up inside Lucan, which was so stupid. These were beginners' clamps! He ignored it and reached for the light switch on the wall so he and Court could see better. Then he lifted up his shirt.

"This is a punishment." Court gave Lucan a dark look. "Do you know what you did?"

Lucan noticed his bottom lip pushing out but let it be. "I didn't text you back."

"No, that's not it."

Lucan's stomach got tight. "Whatever it is, I'm sorry."

"Shh." Court petted through Lucan's hair.

Lucan felt so awkward still holding up his shirt, but Court had given an order, and he hadn't retracted it.

"You didn't tell me you were having sub drop."

Lucan nodded. That made sense. He deserved to be punished.

Arousal had Lucan's nipples hardening, and he reddened in shame.

"It's okay if you like this." Court flicked each of Lucan's nipples, and Lucan's cock filled. "You can get as turned on as you want, but I'm not going to fuck you or make you come."

"Yes, S— Alpha. Yes, Alpha."

Court fumbled with the clamps a bit. But Lucan waited patiently until he got them both on.

"Tighter?" Court asked.

"Yes, Alpha."

Court turned the little silver screws until they couldn't go anymore, meaning they were on the highest setting. The pain was good, perfect. The swell of pain when Court removed them would be even better. And if Court played with them after that... *Fuck.* They would be so sensitive.

Court checked the time on his phone. "All right. Let's cuddle."

Lucan pulled his shirt down. The clamps protruded obscenely, and his nipples and groin both throbbed. He followed after Court like a lost kid, prodding and tugging at his back and arm.

Court was smiling. He kept smiling as they lay down, and his eyes were beautiful. Lucan stroked Court's temple as he stared into the dark depths.

"You're so sweet right now," said Court.

Lucan tensed and hid his face in Court's neck. The movement sent the clamps colliding with Court's body, and Lucan groaned at the half-unpleasant sensation.

"Doing okay?" Court asked.

"Yeah."

"After those clamps come off, you can have a rest; then we'll put them back on."

"No."

"No?" Court stiffened. "Why no? A teaching thing?"

Lucan considered saying that it was, that it wasn't safe, but his conscience wouldn't let him. "Not a teaching thing. It just sounds awful if we won't be doing anything sexual with it."

Court relaxed again and laughed softly. "Tough shit, baby. You need to learn."

"*You* need to learn."

Suddenly, Lucan was on his back, and Court was pushing up his shirt. He held it with an uncomfortable amount of pressure against Lucan's collarbones.

With his free hand, Court checked his phone briefly before setting it on the nightstand. "What happens to mouthy subs? Do you know?"

Heart beating hard, Lucan shook his head.

"Playing dumb looks bad on you." Court very lightly tapped Lucan's cheek, and it was enough of a show of dominance to make Lucan hot all over. He was at Court's mercy, and it was so good, but it was dangerous. He could lose his head... But his head was already lost. They weren't even talking about sub drop anymore.

Court went for the band of Lucan's sweats.

"Wait!" Lucan's rational subconscious sprang forward, and he pried at Court's hands. "We have to do limits first. Please! We have to do cards. Please, please—"

"Okay. Chill." Court climbed off the bed, turning, running his hand through his hair, breathing hard.

Lucan got up, too, and tried to slow his own breathing. He wanted to touch Court, but he couldn't or he'd disappear.

"Do I need to take the clamps off?" Court asked.

"No."

"Tell me what to do." Court actually winced a little after he spoke. It must be hard for him as a Dominant to ask for guidance, but it was mature that he was. Lucan would take it.

He went over to his desk and got out the index cards and a pen. A calm lucidity washed over him as he sat down and wrote two headings on each card: "Soft Limits" and "Hard Limits." Then he wrote Court's name on one, his own name on the other.

"Do you know what limits are?" he asked.

"Stuff you won't do," said Court.

"Right. What about the difference between hard and soft limits?"

"Go ahead and explain it."

"Hard is absolute no-nos. No compromising, no asking, don't even think about it."

Court stood next to Lucan's seated form and put his hand on the back of Lucan's neck. He squeezed, and Lucan's lucidity faltered.

"Please don't touch me right now," said Lucan. "I wanna fucking hump your leg."

Court chuckled and pulled his hand away. "Sorry. Soft limits?"

"You're interested in them, but you're nervous about them or you won't do them except in certain circumstances. There are other reasons. Like, I wouldn't let Dom choke me, but I might let you. 'Cause he's a casual partner, and you're...I don't know."

"You'd better know." Court didn't touch Lucan, but he touched the back of his chair. "You're mine. Right?"

All at once, Lucan remembered his nipples and his cock, and he squirmed in the chair and held his pen too tightly. "I don't know. That's so permanent-sounding."

Court growled. The sound might have been cheesy, but Lucan could tell it came naturally to Court. *Alpha.*

Lucan felt the tip of his cock get wet. "Court, this is serious. We have to focus." He whined and forced himself to stare at the index cards. The only thing working in his favor was that he already knew his limits.

Quickly but neatly, he put scat, piss play, and public humiliation down as hard limits, and blood play, knife play, breath play, and public sex down as soft ones.

The act of writing calmed him down a bit. "Okay. What are yours? It's okay if you don't know them all right now," he added, since Court was new to thinking about BDSM in this way.

Court was silent for a couple of minutes. "I think I know what scat is, and I don't want to do that, either."

Lucan wrote it down. "What else?"

"The diaper thing."

Lucan pressed his lips together to hide a smile. "You mean age play?"

"Yeah. I don't think I want anyone calling me Daddy."

"Hard or soft limit?"

Court was silent again for a few beats. "Soft."

"Okay. Anything else?"

"I don't know."

"You can update this later, and just let me know about it if you do." Lucan wanted to get back to having Court's hands on him, but while he had Court's attention, it was probably a good idea to add something else to their cards. "Then there are must-haves. You won't do a scene without them." Lucan added the heading to each card. Then to his, he wrote aftercare down as a must-have.

"Is submission too obvious as a must-have?" Court asked.

"No." Lucan added it to Court's card. "Some Doms don't want their subs to resist within the scene. You know, be bratty."

"I want you to give it up."

"Yeah." The urge to touch Court was becoming unbearable. *Yes*, Lucan's body was saying. *I'll give it up.*

"And monogamy's one. I don't want you playing with Dom. I don't want you submitting to anyone else, Luc. No one touches you but me."

Lucan wouldn't have liked anyone to know how hot he was for a possessive Dominant, but he was feverish for it. It was difficult to grip the pen, write the word next in Court's must-haves. "I'm sweating here," he said.

"You like that? Being all subby just for me?"

"Yeah. We have to get off tonight, Court." He abandoned the index cards and his pen to look up at Court pleadingly. "I'm so turned on."

Court leaned over Lucan, still not touching, and made a show of reading over the index cards. "I don't see orgasm denial on this list." He tapped Lucan's must-haves. "And I don't see 'getting whatever I want from Court 'cause I'm a whiny baby' on here, either."

Lucan crossed his arms and glared straight ahead. "Screw you."

"Excuse me?" Court yanked Lucan's chair back, which required some strength since it didn't have wheels.

Startled, Lucan gripped the sides of the chair's seat.

"Are we done here?" Court asked. "Can we get back to business?" A rustle, and Court was holding his phone in front of Lucan's eyes. "We're past twenty minutes."

Lucan didn't know what time Court was measuring from, so seeing the stark white numbers didn't tell him much. But he nodded. "Yes, Alpha, just one more thing. For the soft limits, we have to have a little discussion if we want to do any of those. You have to ask first."

"Mhm." Court snatched Lucan's card from the desk and looked it over. "If it's not a soft limit, and it's not on the card, I don't have to ask. Right?"

Lucan swallowed. It felt like he was leaving something out, but he couldn't think what. He just wanted to slip away, fall into Court, become nothing while Court was everything. "Yes, Alpha. You're right."

Overcome, Lucan got out of the chair only to fall to the hardwood floor at Court's feet. He was burning everywhere, throbbing everywhere. He could barely feel his nipples anymore, which couldn't be a good thing, but he found it hard to care. "Take me, use me, punish me. Please, Alpha. Please..."

Court gripped Lucan's hair, sending luscious sparks of pain across his scalp. "Look at you. What a mess." But Court was smiling again. "Let's get those clamps off."

CHAPTER 9

THIS WAS EVERYTHING TO COURT. Lucan in subspace, deferring to Court in all decisions, pawing and clawing and making little sounds.

And though Court didn't want to admit it out loud, that limits card had given him confidence. He'd been confident before—he always was —but now he was *sure* he was making Lucan happy. If Court had been floating on Lucan's doorstep while kissing him goodbye, then he was soaring now—up through the clouds, breaching the atmosphere, utterly free in Lucan's orbit.

"Are you ready?" Court asked, buzzing with anticipation. He and Lucan were sitting face-to-face on the bed, and Court was poised to remove the first nipple clamp.

Lucan nodded.

As soon as Court started unscrewing the clamp, Lucan hissed and took hold of Court's bicep, scratching under the sleeve of his T-shirt. "Fuck, fuck, fuck."

Court liked the bite of pain from Lucan's anguish. It felt right being his scratching post.

By the time Court had gotten the second clamp off, Lucan was a whimpery mess, clinging to Court like he was the only solid thing in a storm.

Gingerly, Court put Lucan on his back and inspected his nipples.

They looked okay—angry but the right shape and color. He was pretty sure he hadn't caused any lasting damage leaving the clamps on longer than planned.

In retrospect, he shouldn't have listened to Lucan when he'd said to leave them on while they talked about limits. Lucan had been biased toward the pleasure—and the pain.

Court licked his thumb and toyed gently with one of the reddened peaks.

Lucan moaned and laid a hand on Court's arm, petting instead of scratching this time.

"Feel good?" Court didn't really need to ask considering Lucan's cock was obviously hard inside his sweatpants, poking obscenely at the light gray fabric.

"Mmm," said Lucan.

Court grinned. How cute was that? Lucan couldn't even talk!

"You have to at least give me a nod, baby," said Court.

Lucan nodded.

"Good boy." Court dipped down and took a nipple in his mouth, sucking and licking. When Lucan moaned some more and squirmed deliciously, Court added gentle bites, then harder ones. The other nipple, he pinched and twisted.

Lucan's moans grew louder, his squirming more insistent.

The power made Court's body hot; his underarms grew damp, and his cock begged for attention. He ignored his own desire and put his mouth on Lucan's other nipple, giving it the same treatment.

Lucan rubbed Court wherever he could reach and murmured unintelligibly, though Court thought he caught a few *Alphas* and *pleases*.

When Lucan's reactions grew less enthusiastic—as Court would expect from the same stimuli over and over—Court sat up and trailed his fingertips from Lucan's throat to his waistband. He longed to test the strength of Lucan's submissive state. What would he allow without any type of protest? The possibilities swirled in Court's head; he knew there were some he wasn't even thinking of. He wished he could keep Lucan in this room for days on end, months. His mind took a dark turn as he imagined Lucan cuffed to the bedpost, his prisoner, his toy.

"Alpha?" Something tickled Court's elbow—Lucan's soft, warm hand.

Court came back to reality—sort of. It felt as if his skin was literally vibrating. "What?" He sounded irritable to his own ears.

"Alpha." It seemed that was the only word Lucan knew. He groped weakly at Court, accomplishing nothing aside from looking desperate and adorable, his gaze big and disoriented.

Court's gaze landed on Lucan's pouty mouth, and at once, he knew what he wanted to do next. He got off the bed and stripped. When he took off his underwear, his erection bounced, and the air kissed its wet tip.

He manhandled Lucan's prone form into the position he wanted: horizontal on the bed, his head dipping a little over the side. With no prompting, Lucan opened his mouth.

"That's right," said Court. "You want to taste me, don't you?"

Lucan grunted and reached back, scratching at Court's thighs.

"Do I need to put mittens on you, kitty cat?" Court had come across those during a Google search. They were called bondage mittens, and they looked like black boxing gloves.

Lucan didn't seem to register the question, or maybe he just didn't care.

Court gripped his dick and slapped Lucan's lips with it. Lucan stuck out his tongue, so Court slapped that, and then he could no longer keep himself from sliding into Lucan's mouth.

This angle was perfect for throat-fucking. Court could feel when the head of his cock passed that ridge at the back of Lucan's mouth, and he thrust lightly, letting it massage his cockhead.

Lucan gave a muffled moan and caressed Court's ass cheek.

"Good boy," Court grunted, and he thrust a little harder. Then, wanting to feel Lucan choke, he pushed as far in as he could go, his balls smashing against Lucan's nose, and he held it.

Lucan gagged, his body jerking with the reflex, and Court pulled all the way out.

Though Lucan coughed and grunted, he still stuck out his tongue, licking air, desperate for more. The power—the utter dominance

Lucan's submission allowed—was like a physical presence across Court's back. *Push it*, his head whispered. *Take him down further. Make him your bitch.*

He remembered the box under Lucan's bed, the one Lucan had let him only get a quick glimpse of.

I shouldn't, Court thought. They hadn't talked about this. But toys *weren't* on Lucan's limits card, and that meant they were free game as long as—

Court went over to check the card again. As long as he didn't use anything in the box to do scat, piss play, or public humiliation, it was allowed. The soft limit of public sex didn't apply here, and he could hold himself back with regard to blood play, knife play, and breath play.

He got on the floor and pulled out the box. It wasn't locked or anything, just latched. The mattress squeaking brought Court's attention back to the bed, where Lucan was peering down at him warily.

"Are you going to pitch a fit about me getting in here?" Court asked.

Lucan shook his head.

But Court wanted to get rid of the worried look still in Lucan's eyes. "You're very cute right now. All quiet and pliable. You're being a very good boy for me."

Lucan smiled shyly and covered his face, and Court's chest swelled with affection. This was where Court always wanted to be—right here in this moment, with power dripping from his fingertips and Lucan's devotion sitting on his head like a crown.

He looked through the box of toys. He had been planning to keep Lucan from orgasming today, but punishing him didn't make sense anymore. They were here in Heaven together, weren't they? It didn't matter that Lucan hadn't answered Court's texts.

Court chose a shiny roll of black bondage tape. He'd seen this in a few porn clips, and he'd actually come jacking off to a GIF on some Tumblr page of a guy penetrating someone with bondage tape on their legs. He tested it to see if he could tear it. Nope. Luckily, Lucan's box also had a pair of scissors. With those, the tape, and the bottle of lube they'd used last time in hand, Court made his way back to the bed.

Lucan inched toward the headboard. "Alpha?"

"Shh, just a little tape. I'm going to put it on your legs." Court yanked Lucan toward him by the ankles and stripped him of his sweats. Naked and lying on his back, Lucan was pliant as Court bent his legs where he wanted them and wrapped them up with the bondage tape. It was a little awkward at first, but Court was no stranger to tape. Though the kind he was used to was for sticking gauze to skin, and the bondage tape only stuck to itself.

Eventually, Lucan was the picture of obscenity with his legs folded and bonded together, leaving him with little to do but spread his legs and show Court his hole.

"Perfect," Court whispered.

"Please." Lucan held his wrists together and jutted them toward Court. Obviously, he wanted them bound as well.

Court obliged. Then he set the tape and scissors safely away and went for the lube.

"You like being bound, huh?" Court hadn't done this with Lucan when they'd dated the first time around, and he'd been missing out. It was truly something to see Lucan displayed for him in this way. What would it be like to wrap him all over in the tape? Then he'd just be an immobile set of holes, a fucktoy with no purpose but to be filled.

Court's erection had flagged a little in his concentration, but now, it grew insistent again, jutting out toward Lucan. He grabbed the lube and, kneeling in front of Lucan, he slicked himself up.

Lucan watched with half-open eyes. It was clear he was barely alert, as if the tightness around his legs and wrists were a drug.

"I'm going to come inside you," Court said.

Lucan might as well have had earmuffs on because he didn't react at all, though he did keep his drugged gaze on Court's.

Court aligned himself and ruthlessly pushed in, knowing Lucan liked the burn.

Lucan offered a soft moan but nothing else.

Court's skin hummed. Lucan's submission was so complete, and he was so hot and tight around Court's swollen dick. Court set a punishing pace, putting all of his frustration into the fucking. Now that Lucan was so deep into subspace that he offered no resistance to anything Court did, the beast inside Court was unleashed. It hadn't made a full appearance for a long while—not for a single guy Court had slammed his cock into since he and Lucan had broken up.

"You were a bad boy for dumping me," he babbled and put a hand on Lucan's neck. He rested it loosely there, didn't squeeze; this was about owning not choking. "I should have found you and fucked you back into submission. I bet you would have thanked me."

Lucan whimpered, and a little crease appeared between his brows.

Court increased the force of his thrusts so that their skin slapped loudly together with each one. "I loved you." His muscles burned as he exerted himself, but he reveled in the pain. "I was going to keep you—" It was hard to get enough air to talk. "—forever."

Lucan stayed limp, his body taking everything Court dished out, but his eyes got a sheen to them, and then a tear leaked out. Court didn't acknowledge it; he just kept thrusting and staring into Lucan's eyes.

At some point, the need for physical release took over, and Court was as lost as Lucan, focusing only on the building pressure in his groin. He wrapped his arms around Lucan's bound legs and used them as handles for pulling him onto his cock. As Court got closer to coming, he thrust deeper and longer. Involuntary growls permeated the bedroom, and Court's whole world became Lucan's yielding body.

With a final, erratic thrust, his balls emptied inside Lucan.

It was a while before Court fell back into the moment. Still holding Lucan's legs, his cock remained seated inside him, and Lucan's own spent cock rested at an angle, cum glistening on his pale stomach.

Lucan watched Court with a little more alertness in his gaze, but he didn't move—not that he could—or speak.

Court reached for some tissues on the nightstand and cleaned them both up. Then he got the scissors and cut off the tape binding Lucan's legs and wrists.

As Lucan stretched out, he moaned softly. Court gathered the supplies and put them back into Lucan's toy box. Once he'd pushed it back under the bed, he rose to find Lucan sitting up, the hard lines of his shoulder blades facing Court.

"That got dark," he said.

Court wasn't sorry. He'd needed to get that out—his resentment. And it wasn't as if he'd hurt Lucan; he'd just fucked him hard, which was what he would have done anyway.

Lucan rested his chin on his shoulder. Again, his eyes were glistening, and big tears fell down his pink cheeks. "I'm sorry," he whispered.

Guilt trickled through Court like ice water. "I didn't mean to make you cry."

"It's fine." Lucan wiped at the tears. "But we have to get tested. We can make an appointment together. Please, Court."

"Yeah, okay." Court realized that was the responsible thing to do, and he didn't want Lucan to worry. He kept mentioning it, so it was obviously important to him. "I used a condom with everybody else. Just so you know."

"That's good." Lucan sniffled and peered over the edge of the bed. Looking for his sweats? "I haven't had sex with anyone in a long time."

"Why not?" Court found Lucan's sweatpants on the floor and tossed them to him. Then he found his own boxer briefs and slipped them back on.

"Nobody does it for me."

"Except me."

"Obviously."

Court smirked. "Don't be a smartass."

Lucan smirked, too. But then a silence descended, and Court wondered if he ought to leave. He reached for his shorts.

"I'm not mad," said Lucan.

"Okay." Court got dressed anyway.

"Seriously. Don't leave." Lucan scurried off the bed and attached himself to Court's side. "You don't have to be anywhere, right? We could watch something on my computer." He kissed Court's jaw sweetly, and it was all very submissive and cute, but Court was hardened to it all of a sudden. He was hardened to Lucan.

"Hey." Lucan took Court's face in his soft hands. His gaze was clear, alert. "Tell me what you need, and I'll give it to you. We went to a painful place in that scene, but I'm here for you."

A tiny weight lifted from Court's shoulders. "Yeah?"

"Aftercare is for both of us. And you were upset when you got here, so..."

Court clenched his jaw. Yeah, he'd been upset. Because when Lucan was unresponsive, it meant he was making decisions about their relationship without Court's involvement, and Court couldn't have that. Not again.

"You have to talk to me, Lucan." Court put their foreheads together. "You have to tell me what's in that crazy head of yours so I can straighten you out when you're wrong."

Lucan chuckled breathily. "When I'm wrong?"

"Yeah, like if you start feeling like I'm not the one for you, because I am." Court pulled Lucan into a tight, almost violent hold. "I'm so scared you'll disappear again." The words hurt coming out, and the back of his throat swelled as if he was going to cry.

Which was ridiculous. He'd just had a great orgasm with the man of his dreams; there was nothing to be upset about.

"I'm yours, Court. It's okay." Lucan wrapped his arms around Court's neck.

"Mine," said Court.

"Maybe... Well, not yet."

"What?" Court pushed Lucan back a little so he could meet his gaze.

Lucan's cheeks flushed deeply. "It's way too soon, but eventually, we could get me a collar."

Court glanced at Lucan's neck, which was really too bare in his opinion. He'd met people at munches who wore collars. One of them had talked so reverently about her shiny, locking one; it was as if she'd been anointed by a god.

"Why not now?" Court asked.

"It's a big commitment."

"Isn't that the point?"

Lucan tried to pull away, but Court held on to him.

Lucan laughed nervously. "People will think I'm fucking crazy."

Court narrowed his eyes. "I'm confused. How do other people's opinions factor into us?"

Lucan's expression radiated fear—like when he'd watched Court from the edge of the bed looking through the toy box. "I do want one. I just... A week ago, I didn't think I'd ever be anyone's submissive."

An immediate urge to protect and reassure strengthened Court's resolve. "You're *my* submissive. You don't have to worry about that anymore."

Lucan smiled in a way that was a little pained. "Let's wait for a bit on the collar. Please." He gave Court a chaste kiss. "I need more time."

Court only nodded; what else could he do? At least Lucan was communicating how he felt.

"Come on." Lucan pulled Court toward the bed. "Let's watch something. Remember that summer when we watched seasons one and two of *Heroes* in like two days?"

Court smiled at the memory. They'd stayed up all night, then taken a break for early-morning donuts, a rare treat for Court. Lucan had gotten a powdered one, and Court could still see him with the white dust on the tip of his nose, eyes crinkled in genuine glee. "Yeah, I remember." He pulled Lucan into a kiss.

Eventually, they got settled side by side on the bed. Lucan's laptop rested on Court's lap and played the pilot of some show they'd found in the Gay & Lesbian section on Netflix. Court really wasn't in the mood to watch anything, but he liked Lucan's head on his shoulder and the fact that Lucan didn't tense or pull away when Court intertwined their fingers.

I love you, he wanted to say. *I never really stopped*. But he knew Lucan wasn't ready to hear it.

CHAPTER 10

IT WAS after midnight by the time Court left. Lucan kissed him goodbye on the stoop amid the mosquitos and fluttering moths and lingered with his palms on Court's strong chest. With Lucan's entire being still yearning to roll over and be good, Court's leaving felt wrong. But the tension that had come between them after they'd had sex hadn't fully dissipated. Court was still giving off negative vibes, his speech and movements tighter and less eager than they'd been the last time they'd seen each other.

"What do you think about going to a play party together soon?" Lucan asked.

"Sure your friends won't make it weird?"

"I'm the one who's been keeping you holed up in my room." Lucan and Court had come down to the kitchen for snacks earlier but had avoided the living room, where Erin, Roland, and Dom had been catching the Summer Olympics. Lucan might have felt left out if he hadn't had Court with him—and if he even remotely enjoyed watching sports (though the swimming portions were worth it for the muscles and Speedos).

"It'll be a good place to formally introduce you to everybody," Lucan added.

"All right." Court cupped Lucan's cheek. "When I check in with you about drop, you'll answer me, right?"

Lucan blushed. "Yes." And he would. Anything to avoid upsetting Court like he had. And he didn't want any punishments, even if Court hadn't actually gone through with the orgasm denial he'd promised. The scene had been painful enough without that, though not in any way Lucan objected to. The only thing that still niggled was that he'd let Court fuck him bare. He'd been in subspace, but not so deeply that he couldn't have said something. Right?

"I want you to address me as Alpha," said Court.

"Shit, sorry. Yes, Alpha."

Court kissed Lucan on the forehead. "Good boy."

The gentle sensation of Court's lips coupled with the words made Lucan tingly. *Please stay the night.* "You're not leaving because I did something bad, are you?" The question sort of fell out, and Lucan grew hot with embarrassment. Why couldn't he just let it be? Court had said he was tired.

"I told you, baby. I have work tomorrow, and I need a good night's sleep."

Lucan wished he hadn't gone so deep into subspace earlier. It had made him feel too open. He had a mental ache he couldn't quite alleviate, and though it was much better than the one he'd had before Court had come over, it was still uncomfortable. Admittedly, he'd probably feel more secure with Court's collar around his neck.

He asked for the next best thing. "Can I list you as my partner on FetNet?" Of course, he still needed to talk to Dom, and the thought made his stomach twist. But he had to tell him before it showed up on everybody's feed. And though Lucan didn't much like having his business everywhere, it would be anyway. As soon as he and Court went to a party together, everybody would gossip. Those who'd seen them together already probably were.

Court smiled, and Lucan's ache lessened. Maybe Court would forget about Lucan dumping him in the past if they moved forward in the present.

"I'd love that." Court kissed Lucan on the lips again. "But now I really gotta go."

Back inside the house, Lucan opened FetNet. Dom was sleeping, so he couldn't update anything yet, but nervous energy had him logging on anyway.

When he got to his page, he froze. He hadn't updated his profile in a while; he mostly used the site to keep track of events. But he knew for a fact he and Dom had had each other listed as play partners just a week ago. Now, Lucan's relationship status said merely "Play Partner" with Dom's username no longer attached.

Lucan shouldn't have been surprised. He shouldn't have been hurt, either; it was what he wanted. But couldn't Dom have given him a heads-up? Just a text, maybe? Even a message on FetNet, as that would have gone to Lucan's email.

Whatever. I'll just add Court now, then.

Anxiety and hurt swirling inside him, Lucan agonized over which FetNet label to give his and Court's relationship. The first part—taking down his "Single" status along with the lonely "Play Partner" one—was easy, but now he had to choose between about fifteen labels. Most of them weren't relevant to him and Court, but the one that was the most relevant—*submissive*—sent a snake of fear and arousal slithering through Lucan's body. "You're *my* submissive," Court had said. But Lucan could choose *bottom* instead. Even *play partner* would be a little bit accurate and might not raise as many brows.

He opted to text Court. He couldn't handle a single other person being mad at him, and Court would be if he picked the wrong thing. *I'm listing you as my Dominant on FetNet. That's what you want, right? You as the Dominant and me as the submissive? There are a few labels to choose from.* He bit his lip and fidgeted with his phone until Court answered.

I know what the other labels are. Yes, those are the correct ones.

Court's authoritative tone translated almost too well to text. Lucan wanted to talk more to him, latch onto that authority like a junkie to a fix. But he needed to let Court sleep—and he needed to stop being so shameless.

He listed himself as Court's submissive. Almost immediately, Court approved the connection, and then there the twin notifications sat on the public feed. In unassuming, white sans serif font against FetNet's signature black background, they read: "bottleblond4837 added a new relationship: submissive of MisterK289" and "MisterK289 added a new relationship: Dominant of bottleblond4837." The public claiming made everything more real. Lucan wasn't Dom's casual play partner anymore. He had a Dominant who liked what he liked, fucked him hard, punished and praised him.

He had Court back. This was his life now.

It took Lucan a long time to fall asleep. When he woke in the morning, it was to an influx of comments on his FetNet wall. "Congratulations!" "Oh my gosh, who's MisterK?" "What????!!!!! I thought you'd never!" "I'm so happy for you." "Who is he?? Jealous!" "What about Dom?"

In the harsh light of day, the changed relationship status was a lot less comforting. He should have known better than to check FetNet first thing.

Groaning, Lucan hugged his pillow and went back to sleep.

* * *

Almost two weeks went by before Lucan saw Court again, but Court did text to check in about drop. Lucan definitely didn't experience any this time, though he wondered about Court. For a few days after they saw each other, Court's texts were short and to the point—no flirting. But once they decided on the party they would go to together—the next TNG party—Court got back to his usual self, sending Lucan links and pictures pertaining to the things he wanted to do.

Lucan tried to influence him to keep it simple. He didn't think it was a great idea for Court to play publicly yet, but Court didn't seem to be hearing him whenever Lucan expressed that.

We don't have to use any toys. I can just spank you. Or you can blow me.

Lucan got *that* reply during one of his fifteen-minute breaks at work, and it took thirteen of the fifteen to compose himself before he went back to his customers.

I'm not going to blow you in front of a bunch of people, Court. I've barely blown you in private

We'll take care of that.

By the time the night of the party rolled around, Lucan was jonesing for his submissive hit, and he was a little closer to letting Court do whatever he wanted to him—spanking, demanding a blow job, whatever. He had long grown to recognize the agitation, frayed emotions, and desperate thoughts as his brain's way of telling him it was time to find a safe person to let go with.

For so long, Lucan's safe person had been Dom—though he'd never fully *let go* with him. When Roland let Lucan know that Dom wasn't planning to attend the night's party, Lucan found himself pounding on Dom's closed bedroom door.

When Dom answered, he appeared as his usual calm self, though he raised his eyebrows at Lucan. "Wow. You look great."

Lucan ignored the compliment. "Hey, is this because of me?"

"What? Me not going to the party?"

"Yeah."

Dom shrugged. "A little."

The admission gave Lucan nothing to work with. "I said I was sorry, Dom."

"And I said 'a little.' It's not all about you." Dom leaned against the doorjamb and crossed his arms. "You finding someone gave me room to think about some things is all."

Lucan didn't bring up how shitty it was that Dom hadn't shared any of this with him earlier. He'd just clammed up, and then he'd changed their relationship status on FetNet without consulting Lucan at all. "What kinds of things?"

"Remember when we first met? I told you I was planning on leaving the lifestyle."

Lucan's already heightened nerves buzzed with panic. "You can't leave."

"Relax, I didn't say I was leaving. I'm just thinking things over. Reassessing."

Lucan hugged himself. "What's that mean?"

Dom sighed through his nose. "I need to figure out what I want. Do I want another arrangement like you and I had? Do I want a submissive? Do I want to find a nice vanilla someone to settle down with? I'm twenty-nine. It's time to grow up and figure this shit out."

Most of what Dom was saying made sense, but Lucan still had the sinking feeling that he was going to lose him. "You can settle down with someone in the lifestyle."

"Yeah, I guess."

Lucan picked at the doorjamb.

"Come here," said Dom.

"Hmm?" Lucan looked up, and Dom was pulling him into a hug all of a sudden. The affection was welcome and unwelcome at the same time, and Lucan tensed. But when Dom didn't budge, Lucan wrapped his arms around his solid frame. Maybe Dom didn't project the type of forceful authority that got Lucan so worked up, but he had that indescribable quality that all true Dominants had. He gave off a vibe of assurance that everything was going to be fine as long as you listened to him. Lucan trusted him completely, and he realized in a fresh, painful way that he still didn't have that trust with Court.

He might not ever feel this sure with him. The fear choked him.

He clutched Dom tighter. "Don't disappear from the lifestyle like some people do and then never talk to me again."

Dom rubbed Lucan's back. "You have a shitty opinion of me if you think I would do that to you."

"Sorry."

They disentangled, and Lucan figured he should go wait for Roland and Erin downstairs. But something kept him where he was, even though the awkwardness was palpable.

"I saw your update on Fet," said Dom.

"I saw *your* update." Lucan flushed after the words escaped him; he didn't need to be passive-aggressive like that. "I mean, I saw you removed me."

Dom averted his gaze for a second. "I was mad."

"I know."

"I can put it back if you still plan on playing with me. But you don't, do you?"

Sheepishly, Lucan shook his head. "I was going to talk to you about it."

"So, we're talking now. It's not a big deal."

Lucan and Dom had scened together once or twice a month—almost every month—for years. It *was* a big deal to Lucan. But he just nodded.

Dom touched him under the chin, pulling Lucan's gaze to his. "Don't let Court walk all over you just because he turns you on. I can see how submissive he makes you feel. You're not acting like you usually do right now."

The blunt, unexpected words were like a bucket of ice water over Lucan's head. He squared his shoulders. "What?"

"You heard me." Dom smiled, maybe to soften his words. "I'm just looking out for you."

"I'll be fine."

Dom squeezed Lucan's shoulder. "Have fun at the party."

Five minutes later, Lucan was getting into the back seat of Roland's car.

Erin peeked past the passenger's seat at him, her hair in a big pink ribbon. "What's wrong?"

"Nothing," said Lucan.

"Are you and Dom still fighting?"

"No, we're good."

Erin frowned but let it go.

Lucan tried to swallow the trepidation creeping up his throat. Everything was going to be okay. He wasn't losing control of himself. He wasn't becoming a submissive mess with no judgment or instinct for safety. He wasn't a sub with years in the BDSM lifestyle getting that frowned-upon newbie sub frenzy because of one uneducated Dominant.

Trying to quiet his inner turmoil, Lucan sent Court a text. *On our way to the party. You there yet? Can't wait to see you*

* * *

Court actually choked on his drink when he spotted Lucan coming into the kitchen. It was like they were back in college again and about to go to the club except Lucan had upgraded—significantly. Where he'd used to wear the same pair of black skinny jeans all the time with a slew of graphic tees, tonight, the skinny pants were vinyl and metallic gold, and the tees had been exchanged for a skin-tight black tank with open sides. Only a few strips held the garment together with Lucan's skin on display between them. Court wanted to stroke those ribs, make Lucan shudder.

Lucan spotted Court and grinned before making his way over to the table where Court sat. "Hey." Even his jewelry did it for Court. A little gold ring glinted at his septum, and his earlobes were heavy with black horseshoe barbells.

Court's hungry gaze finally landed on Lucan's eyes. "Are you wearing eyeliner?" *Fuck.* Court loved that little hint of femme style.

Lucan's smile faltered. "Do you hate it? I never—"

"I love it." Court pulled Lucan closer by one of the straps on that slutty tank and play-bit at his arm.

Lucan giggled and pulled away. "Stop it."

"So this is the guy?"

The unfamiliar, smooth male voice had a feral urge to claim going through Court. He held Lucan next to his sitting form with a possessive arm around his waist.

The voice belonged to a light-skinned black man with the most perfect bone structure Court had ever seen.

"Yeah, this is Mister K," said Lucan.

"Court, actually. You are?"

The guy's easy demeanor didn't falter. "I go by Flame here."

"Nice to meet you."

"Likewise. Lucan's been evading all of us for a while. Can't believe you snatched him up so quick."

Court bared his teeth in a grin. "We go way back."

"Stop it, Court," Lucan whispered and nudged Court's shoulder.

Court asked at full volume, "Stop what?"

"You might as well be growling."

That's why you need a collar. Keep the dogs away. "It's my first event with him as mine," Court said half-apologetically, but for Lucan's sake only.

"I get it," said Flame. "You guys are monogamous. That's cool."

"Want to go to the playroom?" Lucan asked in a sweet, submissive voice.

At the chance to escape, Court stood, and he and Lucan headed out of the kitchen's bright light and into the playroom. The overhead lights had been covered with red paper, lending the whole area a moody glow, and dark pop music vibed through the space. Lucan tugged Court toward a big couch. Once Court was seated, he pulled Lucan onto his lap, and there was something deliciously illicit about having Lucan sit on him like a child would.

But Lucan wasn't a child. Holding him around the waist, Court pressed his nose against Lucan's neck and breathed in, picking up a sweet, fresh scent that was probably Lucan's body wash. It made him forget they were in a public place, and he snaked his hand down between Lucan's legs, palming his dick through the stiff, vinyl fabric of those ridiculous pants.

Smoothly, Lucan took Court's hand and brought it back to his waist. He held it there and interlocked their fingers.

Court felt like a ferocious dog who'd just been yanked back by his leash, and it sucked. Why had they come to this party again? Why did they need to be around these people? Distantly, he recognized his thoughts weren't entirely rational, but irritability still fell over him like a heavy blanket. For the past couple of weeks, he'd been excited about doing a scene here, but now he didn't know how to go about it. Lucan had kept shooting him down. Court had asked him to bring his toy bag, and he'd said it was too much of a hassle. So Court had mentioned spanking, a blow job—things they didn't need toys for. Lucan had shot those ideas down, too.

Court had thought maybe Lucan would budge in person. Then he'd stopped worrying about it because he'd just wanted to see Lucan—at the end of those two weeks, he'd really started to miss him. Now, being in the same room with him was not enough. Having Lucan sit on him and hold his hand was not enough.

Court grazed the side of Lucan's neck with his teeth. "Let's go somewhere."

"Shh. We're not supposed to talk in the playroom."

The beast that Court always carried around inside him vibrated with the urge to satisfy itself—and punish Lucan for being so disrespectful.

"Am I your Dom or not?" Court whispered. "Address me correctly, and don't ever shush me."

Lucan stiffened for a second, then patted Court's forearm. "Sorry, Alpha."

Even that irked Court. What was wrong with him? Maybe he should tell Lucan he wasn't feeling the party and leave. But what would that accomplish? He'd be alone at home and still without the stimulation he craved.

A memory surfaced from back at school. He'd been sitting in the living room at his apartment trying to focus on a writing assignment. He'd hated essays—nothing more boring to write and read. And all he'd been able to think about was Lucan and shoving him down and taking him.

It hadn't been a good yearning he'd felt. The assignment was a big one. The composition class was a requirement, and if he got anything less than a C-, he'd lose his scholarships. So an hour later, when he still only had the introduction written and Lucan texted him (*Give me an order so I can disobey it ;)*), Court shut off his phone. He couldn't have his relationship with Lucan—no matter how hot it was—interfere with his future.

In the present, Court's frustration grew stormier. He felt the same now as he'd felt back then, but he didn't have anything stopping him from indulging in Lucan except Lucan himself. Court didn't need these people to watch. He'd happily take Lucan to his car again despite the cramped space.

Court said a little above a whisper, "I want you. Let's go somewhere."

"There's a scene I want to see."

Court rolled his eyes. What could be more exciting than Lucan's submission to Court? "What scene?"

Lucan pointed to a massage table a few feet in front of them where a topless female bottom wearing nothing but a pair of sheer stockings was getting settled on her stomach. A heavyset woman in a corset stood nearby.

"Hannah does knives," Lucan whispered.

Court assumed Hannah was the heavyset woman. On a little table, she unfurled a roll of fabric, and several tools glinted from little pockets inside.

Lucan looked back at Court over his shoulder. "Usually people use dull knives, but Hannah doesn't."

Court licked his lips. "She's going to cut her?"

Lucan nodded. "May we watch, Alpha?"

It was the right way to ask. "Sure."

From a big toy box on the floor, Hannah got a pair of latex gloves and snapped them on. Then she retrieved a bottle of something and wiped down her play partner's back. Court guessed it was rubbing alcohol.

The bottom wiggled her stocking-covered toes as Hannah went back to her set of knives. After some consideration, she slid out a small one. It was hard for Court to see details, but it wasn't an everyday kitchen knife. It was a little smaller than a paring knife, and its handle had holes in it.

Court was ready to see a cut. He wanted to see that line of blood bead up, see the bottom eat up the pain. The memory of Lucan's stomach fluttering under several shallow cuts appeared behind Court's eyes, and he held Lucan more tightly around the waist. Lucan had let go of Court's hand by now, but he found it again and squeezed and rubbed it. Was he having the same memory?

Hannah built up the anticipation for her bottom, running the blade along the back of her neck, down her shoulder blades, across her waist where the stockings began. When Hannah ran the blade up the bottom's thigh and let it dip just barely between her legs, the bottom wiggled, and Court's stomach tightened. He'd never touched Lucan below the waist with a blade, but now he wanted to.

The first cut came down the bottom's back. Court resisted the urge to push Lucan off and get closer because it would be useless. He wouldn't be able to get close enough to hear the bottom's subtle noises —any moans, whimpers, quick or heavy breaths. He wouldn't be able to touch her body, see if it trembled or tensed.

Court wasn't interested in having sex with women, but that was irrelevant here. The scene was about power, and Hannah wielded complete control over the girl under her blade.

Hannah made more cuts. The bottom's toes curled, and her hands, where they lay next to her hips on the massage table, opened wide, then closed into fists. She must be so turned on, wet inside those stockings.

Mentally, Court put Lucan in her place, stockings and all. So what if they were for girls? He'd look beautiful in them.

Hannah chose a different knife. This one was a little bigger with a more substantial handle, and she dragged the blade across the back of each of the bottom's knees and along the inside of each thigh. Then she put it between her legs and actually pushed the blade into the stockings —into her pussy.

A intense wave of arousal hit Court's groin. Lucan was the one who was all about safety, but a knife in the pussy? That seemed risky beyond belief.

But Hannah didn't keep it there. She set the knife aside and shoved her gloved fingers through the cut she'd made in the stockings, finger-fucking the bottom with no gentleness. The girl moaned loudly enough for everyone to hear, and Court glanced away for a couple of seconds to find that most of the people in the dungeon were now watching. The public interest added a level of intensity to the scene that had Court's mouth going dry.

The bottom was shameless now, wiggling and gripping the massage table and pushing back against the fingers inside her. Court had never been so captivated by a woman writhing in pleasure. His own groin throbbed, his cock hardening.

Lucan's hand came down onto the arm of the couch at their side, but otherwise, he remained infuriatingly still on Court's lap.

Court put his hand on Lucan's stomach where he'd used to cut him years ago. "Let me do that to you tonight."

Without looking away from the scene, Lucan said, "Finger me?"

"Cut you."

The bottom humped the massage table with increasing ferocity. Large runs marred her stockings now, blooming from where Hannah continued to finger-fuck her. Court didn't blink—it seemed no one in the dungeon did as they all watched the girl's movements get more and more out of control. Then she tensed up, cried out, and jerked. Once she'd gone still again, Hannah removed her hand, then the gloves.

A third person joined them to help the bottom off the massage table, and an irregular, wet smear glinted from the table's vinyl where the girl's pussy had obviously been. It was the most erotic thing Court had ever seen. He understood now why Lucan had wanted to stay and watch, but now, the scene was over.

Court snaked a hand over Lucan's throat and spoke into his ear. "I wanna make you shiver under a blade. Let's go to your place."

In Court's loose hold, Lucan turned his head. "We can't."

"Why not?"

"Dom's there. He'll hear us."

"I'll gag you."

"No." Lucan furrowed his brow. "I'm not letting you gag me *or* cut me, Court."

Something inside Court cracked, and he took his hands off Lucan to prevent himself hurting him. "Get off me, then."

Uncertainty clouded Lucan's expression, but he got up.

Court shouldered past him and out of the playroom. It wasn't a quick or smooth exit because the party was packed now, but in a couple of minutes, he'd made it outside. A few people chatted at the front of the house. Court walked past them as well and headed for his car parallel parked down the street.

Over and over, he had the same awful thought: *Lucan isn't really mine.*

He got into his car and pulled the door closed with too much force.

Court had thought Lucan was his again—Lucan had said it a few times by now—but Court could see that it wasn't true. Yes, he'd allowed Court to fuck him and dominate him, but it had been a battle every time. Court had been trying to battle for it again tonight, but Lucan was a wall of resistance now. Probably, he was regretting this whole thing with Court and just not saying so because that was what he did.

Court had been fine without Lucan. Dating had sucked because he'd been looking for someone with the same tastes and never found him, but he'd had hope he might in the BDSM community. He could still find someone else. So why was panic dripping into him like a poison? Why couldn't he breathe?

His phone buzzed in his pocket: a text from Lucan. *Please come back inside*

Court's fingers flew over the screen. *Why should I?*

Because I want you to. Please, Alpha

The honorific felt manipulative in this moment—not sexy or respectful. *Not good enough. I'm tired of being rejected. You don't want to do what we used to do, but I love those things. What's the point of getting back together? You hold me back. It's bullshit. You don't care about my feelings.*

The words came from a part of him he hadn't connected with in a long time. He sent the text, but reading over it, he felt like a huge bruise that Lucan was poking.

He shouldn't have sent it. He should go home. He needed a drink.

Seems to me you're throwing a tantrum because I won't let you cut me

The words made Court burn in the worst way. This wasn't a tantrum. This wasn't just about the damn knives!

You've shot me down on a bunch of stuff besides that.

I'm not ready to do some things. You have to respect MY feelings on that.

What are you ready for? Vanilla fucking? I can get that from anyone. Court knew the words were cruel, but they were true, so he sent them anyway.

Lucan didn't seem fazed. *Right, cause spanking, bondage tape, and me calling you Alpha is vanilla as hell*

It's not enough. Court wished he could explain it better. But while that other stuff did it for him, he was ready for more now. Edgier play —*real* punishments, knives, blood—was what would really bring Lucan back to him.

I don't know what to tell you, said Lucan.

You aren't mine. I can't feel you like before. I still miss you.

There. Maybe that would do it. But now Court's eyes were stinging.

After a few minutes, Lucan hadn't replied, and Court couldn't stop himself from sending another text.

I don't know what you're so afraid of. I won't hurt you. I'm a fucking EMT! He threw his phone into the passenger's seat and gave the steering wheel a smack.

Why did Lucan have to make everything so difficult?

CHAPTER 11

COURT'S TEXTS did awful things to Lucan. He was on the front porch where people weren't really supposed to sit, curled up on the wooden swing with his phone the only light aside from one dim bulb under the awning. He'd gone out here for the privacy. No one needed to see him being a nervous wreck, and besides, all those people inside knew by now that Court was Lucan's new Dominant. They might ask him about it like Flame had. And what would Lucan say? *Yeah, he was here, but he left. He's mad at me. We might still be together by the next party, but at this rate, who knows?*

One particular text echoed in Lucan's head over and over: *You aren't really mine.*

Lucan knew Court didn't mean it literally. But the submissive part of him took the words like a punishment. Lucan didn't please his Dominant tonight, so he didn't get to hear any proud, possessive words. Instead, he got abandoned.

Lucan should have put mind games on his limits list. He remembered that Court had listed it as a fetish on his FetNet profile. Was that what this was? Lucan didn't think so. It was Court being upset he wasn't getting to do whatever he wanted as the Dominant. But that wasn't how things worked in safe, sane, and consensual BDSM, and Lucan had good reasons for refusing to do knife play.

Right? Like the fact that it was dangerous, and Court didn't listen enough, and Lucan had *no* hope of staying alert. He'd go so deep into subspace he wouldn't be able to see the end until days later.

I don't know what you're so afraid of, Court had texted last. *I won't hurt you. I'm a fucking EMT!*

He had a point. An EMT could still get too Top-high to make good decisions, like when he'd fucked Lucan bare last time. But in a crisis, he'd be an asset. In a *physical* crisis, like if he cut Lucan too deep. For most submissives, that was their biggest fear, but not Lucan's. Court wasn't an idiot. He wouldn't injure him. The thing that scared Lucan the most was the possibility of being broken again.

It had been horrible last time. Maybe for some people, breakups didn't feel like a war to survive, crawling out from under piles of dead bodies just trying to breathe. But it had taken months of therapy for Lucan to see clearly again. It had only been because of that therapy that Lucan hadn't begged Court back. The counselors at the university health center had convinced him that Court had been abusive. Lucan didn't think that was the right word. But he hadn't been happy with him —not for the majority of the time.

He wasn't happy now.

God, *why* had he done this? Why had he let Court back in so easily? He'd been comfortable with Dom. He went to work, he came home, he wrote a few BDSM-related articles for a few dollars, and he went to parties and played with Dom. Easy. Calm. Now Dom didn't even know if he wanted to be in the community at all, and Court was after Lucan like a hound who'd scented blood.

Why had Lucan been so stupid?

I was bored. The revelation was like a streak-free swipe through the grime on a dirty window, but the sun that shone through the glass hurt Lucan's eyes. Had it really been boredom that had driven him back here? Had he wanted a little excitement so badly that he'd let the one man who'd ever really gotten to him back under his skin?

Yes. Because sensation play wasn't really his fetish. Because Dom always used the same toys, and when he hadn't—that one time he'd used knives—Lucan had had to put a stop to it. The truth was he couldn't have a true thrill or deep subspace without devotion forming in his heart. Some people could, but not Lucan. At least, he didn't think so, and he'd always been too scared to try.

Court wanted Lucan's devotion, though. That was what he'd meant when he'd said Lucan wasn't his. *I can't feel you like before*, he'd said. *I still miss you.* When Court had come over and put those nipple clamps on him, he'd gone pretty deep into it, but not as deep as he'd used to. He'd still held back.

Part of him wondered if he could actually get there even if he tried. What if these years of keeping himself locked up had done damage, too?

That line of thinking had an uncomfortable dissonance vibrating through his brain. His thoughts were getting out of control, folding in on themselves. As he'd been told to do in therapy countless times, he focused instead on the present moment. *I'm sitting on a wooden porch swing. Its metal squeaks when I move. It's dark outside. The air is warm. My clothes are tight. I hear gravel crunching in the distance. A car. It's gone now.*

When he felt sufficiently anchored to reality, he asked himself: *What do I want?* The answer was Court. Pain, submission, pleasure, aftercare. He wanted to lose control at Court's hand and fall into bliss with him. Afterward, he wanted to cuddle in those strong arms against that strong, safe body and drift to sleep knowing he was owned. That he had a home for that soft, scared part of himself that he'd been building walls over ever since Court had touched him there and left wounds.

The wounds were healed over, but scar tissue was sensitive. If he and Court were going to play how they really wanted to, Lucan had to make sure Court understood what Lucan needed.

He sent Court a text: *Did you go home?* If he had, maybe he'd be willing to double back and get Lucan.

No. I'm sitting in my car.

Lucan let out a breath. He got up and ventured away from the house, looking through the cars parallel parked along the road for

Court's black one. It wasn't easy to spot him, as he was sitting in the dark, but eventually, he did.

He knocked on the passenger's-side window.

Court startled and unlocked the car.

Lucan got in. "Okay, here's the thing."

"What?" Court asked in a rough voice.

"We can do knives, but you have to *promise* me you'll be there for me. For one—"

"I'm there for you! Have I not been there for you?"

"Let me finish." Lucan waited until he was sure Court was ready to listen. "For one, no more bareback until I have paper proof in my hands that we're both clean. And for two, if I go all in on this, I'm done for. I have to know you're all in, too. I know you're not going to hurt me too badly where knives are concerned. I trust you there. But my head, my emotions..." Lucan swallowed, ignoring the swell of feeling trying to suffocate him. "Please take care of me. Please don't make me feel like I don't have anybody when I'm supposed to have someone." His eyes welled a little, but no tears fell. Lucan was proud himself.

"Okay..." Court sounded unsure.

"What?" Lucan asked.

"I have work. I lock up my personal phone during work. It's the rules, so I—"

"I'm not crazy. I get you might not be able to talk to me every minute." Lucan would prefer that—he wouldn't lie—but work was work. "I have a job, too."

"I know."

Feeling naked and awkward, Lucan focused on the bland view out the window. Just grass and gravel, barely perceptible in the darkness.

Court took Lucan's hand, pulling his attention back. "You can't bail on me."

The part of Lucan that was obsessed with doing BDSM correctly wanted to tell Court that he could break up with him whenever he wanted and he would just have to deal with that. But he understood that Court needed reassurance. "I won't bail." *I'll take care of you, too.*

"Okay." Court took a deep breath. "You're worried about Dom being home. Do you want to go to my place?"

"Sure. Do you have...supplies?"

"Knives, you mean? Yeah, I think I can find something." Court brought Lucan's hand to his lips and watched him out of the tops of his eyes. Lucan was used to kink, but that contrast—Court talking about cutting him while performing such a charming gesture—got him in the groin.

Lucan took a calming breath, and Court's eyes twinkled like he knew exactly what he was doing to him.

"Let's go, then," Lucan said. As Court started the car and pulled onto the road, Lucan sent a text to Roland. *Leaving with Court. Probably won't be home until tomorrow.*

* * *

Lucan wished he could feel submissive on command. Not even a command from Court—just his own internal decision should do it. But following Court inside his apartment, he felt outside of the moment again, and he was having trouble getting back into it. *I'm walking on carpet. It's...beige, I think? Court's in front of me. We're in a hallway. I'm—*

"Oh." Lucan hesitated in front of a door that had light coming from beneath it. "You live with somebody?"

"My sister. You remember Cally?" Court asked.

Lucan had met her a couple of times over school breaks when he and Court had dated. Being Court's twin, she had gone to college at the same time but at Bryn Mawr.

"Yeah. I don't know how this is better than being at my place with Dom, though." Lucan crossed his arms.

"Uh, the difference is Cally doesn't give a shit. We have a code."

Lucan raised his eyebrows. "A code?"

"Yeah. I send her a text, and she puts her earbuds in."

"How many guys have you brought back here?"

Court laughed. "Enough. Come on."

Lucan resumed following Court. What kind of guys had Court brought back here? Submissive ones? Masochists?

Court led him into a room farther down and flicked on the light. "This is my bedroom. Wait for me here." He slapped the doorjamb before scurrying away.

Lucan felt vaguely nauseous and tried to distract himself with snooping.

Court's room held a king-sized bed and not much else; there just wasn't room. A small bookshelf and a nightstand left enough space to walk along each side of the bed. Then there was a closet, open to reveal messily hung clothes and a cluttered overhead shelf. The biggest open space lay between the closet and the foot of the bed.

Lucan sat on the bed so he could check out the books. An EMT Basic exam guide, a medical textbook, and a huge paperback called *Best Gay Love Stories 2016*. Lucan smirked and reached out for that one.

The lights went out. Lucan froze, blinked.

It seemed to happen all at once: a squeak and dip of the mattress, a solid body pressing against his back, a knife at his throat.

"Court?" Lucan choked out.

"What's my name?" Court asked.

Warmth pooled in Lucan's groin. "Alpha."

"That's right." Court removed the knife but immediately yanked Lucan back to lie on the mattress.

Lucan helped Court position him vertically on the bed.

"I think we'll stick with Alpha. Do you like that, baby?" Court asked.

"Yeah. Feels right."

"I agree." Court switched on the bedside lamp.

Lucan could see now that he was wearing a ski mask. But he peeled it off, revealing a giant grin and adorably mussed hair.

Lucan's dick twitched. "Should I take my clothes off?" He should have waited for orders, but when he was nervous, the words just fell out.

"No, just relax. I'll undress you."

"Okay."

"You're not relaxing."

"Sorry. Is that knife sharp?" *Please cut me fast. Make me shut up.*

Court chuckled. "Yes, Lucan. Should I prove it to you?"

"Yes," Lucan replied eagerly.

Court tossed the knife on the bed and took his shirt off. Saliva bloomed on Lucan's tongue at the sight of those muscles. Instinctively, he spread his legs, pulling the stiff fabric of his metallic jeans tighter against his cock.

To Lucan's surprise, Court straddled him. After grabbing the knife, he snapped his fingers in front of his stomach, drawing Lucan's gaze. Then he drew the knife across his own flesh.

Blood sprouted up along the cut, and Lucan breathed through his mouth. He'd never had anyone do this for him, and he was more into it than he would have expected, though his stomach clenched with the urge to take Court's place under the blade.

"See?" Court swiped his finger through the blood and transferred it to Lucan's jawline. "Sharp."

Lucan moaned. He'd have to add a new fetish to his FetNet profile: *my Dom's blood on my skin*. But other people might not understand this, not even knife play enthusiasts.

Court set the flat part of the blade against Lucan's cheek. "You're going to show me everything tonight. No secrets. No walls." Hesitation must have shown in Lucan's eyes because Court moved the blade to this throat, pressing the side in. Lucan couldn't tell if it was the sharp edge or the dull one.

Court pressed the sweetest of kisses between Lucan's brows. "Something else you're worried about?"

"What if I can't?" Lucan's voice came out small and frightened, and he hated himself for it. He just wanted to be good for Court; instead, he was being a pain in the ass.

Court sighed through his nose, and the disappointment there pricked Lucan like thorns. "I'm asking you to try, that's all. Will you do that for me?"

The way he asked it was so earnest that an unbearable urge to touch and comfort hit Lucan, so he set his hand on Court's forearm. "Yes, Alpha. I'll try."

"Good boy." Court gave Lucan another forehead kiss and removed the blade. He set it aside and did as he'd promised, undressing Lucan to his black and mesh boxer briefs pulled taut over his erection.

Court traced a seam in the material. "I like these."

"Thank you."

"I don't suppose you'd like it if I cut them and finger-fucked you through them?"

The submissive in Lucan wanted to say he didn't mind, but these underwear had cost him like sixteen dollars just for the one pair. "Please don't."

"I'm only joking, Luc. You don't have to be so serious about this."

"Just hurt me already." The words were out of line; Lucan knew as soon as he'd spoken them, but the sudden snap of Court's gaze onto his told him, too.

"Don't test me," said Court.

It was on Court's limits card that he needed a willing sub. No brats.

Lucan righted himself. "I'm sorry, Alpha. The pain will help me relax. I need it. Please." He could feel himself sinking into the correct headspace; relief from his worries was so close. *Hand it over to Court. Hand it all over to Court.*

"I like hearing you beg."

"Please."

"Don't overdo it. Don't be pathetic."

Lucan made a little noise. That talk, a touch degrading... It was like pain.

"Alpha." Lucan moaned the word.

"I'm here." Finally, Court took the knife in hand again and, kneeling next to Lucan on the big bed, ran the sharp side of the blade very lightly across his shoulder. It tickled, and Lucan shivered.

Court teased him all over this way. Collarbones, nipples, ribs, hip bones. He even tickled Lucan's palms, trailing the blade down the underside of each finger.

Lucan floated in the sensations like he had with Dom, shuddering and squirming under tickling feathers, riding crops, Wartenberg wheels. It wasn't the high he craved from Court, but it was pleasant. He only tensed up when it was involuntary, his body and psyche riding the waves of sensation with ease.

Then Court slid a strong hand around Lucan's face. "Come back."

It was as if Court had spoken a hypnotist's cue to bring Lucan out of a trance. He opened his eyes and focused every bit of his awareness on Court.

"How do you feel?" Court asked.

"Green." The answer was automatic.

A crease came between Court's brows, but then he smiled. "Ah, right. Green for 'keep going.'"

Lucan nodded.

Court kissed him. It was too short—just a peck—and Lucan whined.

"Green," he tried.

Court's eyes gleamed. "I adore you." It felt like *I love you*.

Lucan's heart lifted. "Alpha."

"I'm gonna hurt you now."

Yes, please.

Court ran a hand down Lucan's stomach, the warm, heavy touch grounding him, keeping him in his body. Lucan didn't worry about what he needed anymore; Court was going to give it to him.

The blade glinted in the lamplight. Court brought it down against Lucan's skin and pressed, pulled. A delicate sting radiated from the little wound, and Lucan watched his own blood bead across it.

Court made another cut, then another. Was he spelling something? Lucan craned to look, but Court pushed him down. Then Lucan was forced to focus on the sensations, and he squirmed even though he knew it was dangerous to move like that under a sharp knife.

"Stay still," Court warned, "or next time I'll strap you down."

"Sorry, Alpha."

"I can tell you aren't sorry."

A nervous feeling fluttered through Lucan at having been found out. "No, I am, Alpha. I promise."

"You're lying. Do I have to punish you every time we're together?"

Lucan clammed up.

A moment later, and Court was finished with whatever he'd been carving into Lucan.

"May I look?" Lucan asked.

"Yes."

Lucan slid off the bed, and Court led him to the closet, where he pulled the sliding door closed to reveal a mirror.

The letters were jagged, like a little kid had drawn them, but they clearly spelled out "COURT" in red lines above the band of Lucan's underwear.

Lucan's heart raced, and he tingled all over. Court had *marked* him. Claimed him.

Court dropped to his knees behind Lucan.

Lucan started. "What are you—?"

Court yanked down Lucan's underwear, spread his ass cheeks, and rimmed him.

Lucan gasped. The hot, wet sensation was amazing on its own, but watching Court in the mirror on his knees for Lucan, servicing him, did something to Lucan's head that made this so much better. Court wasn't submissive the way he did it. This was him taking control of Lucan's pleasure, and he was deliciously confident about it.

Court worked his tongue until he was spearing Lucan's hole. Lucan whimpered and struggled to stay upright. With nothing else nearby to hold on to for support, he leaned on Court's shoulders and fought the urge to push against his mouth.

Lucan's cock curved up toward the letters carved into his flesh. It was a deep red, with the flush spreading out around it, decorating Lucan's pale skin. For Court, Lucan's body bloomed like a flower, and Lucan was fixated on the reflection of them. He watched precum swell at the tip of his cock.

"Alpha." He choked the word; the onslaught was never ending! Then Court added his fingers, stretching Lucan wider, tonguing him deeper.

Lucan's stomach muscles tightened, making the cuts sting anew. His balls pulled up toward his body, and he watched his cock twitch, once, twice—

"Alpha!" Instinctively, Lucan tried to pull away from Court, but Court wouldn't let him, vicing his legs in twin holds as he continued to rim and lick and tongue-fuck.

In his way, Lucan had warned Court that he would come from this, and apparently, Court was fine with it. He thrust his fingers into Lucan like Hannah had done to her submissive. On each pump, Lucan begged silently for orgasm. He was so close, teetering right on the edge...

Court had the knife again—where had it come from? One hand still impaling Lucan, he brought the knife to Lucan's thigh.

Lucan almost forgot about the fingers in his ass as his focus narrowed to that glinting blade in the mirror's reflection. It was cool against his skin and sharp when Court turned it and pressed and dragged. The cut was a little deeper than the ones on his stomach, and it hurt so good, so good...

Lucan came, splattering the mirror with his cum.

Court tossed the knife away just in time to catch Lucan as he lost the ability to stand. They tumbled to the floor together, and Court pushed Lucan onto his back. Shoving down his pants just enough to get his cock out, Court gripped himself and stroked roughly, his face squeezed into a pained expression.

Feeling sated and devoted, Lucan mumbled to try and help get Court off. "Come on me, Alpha. Please. You cut me so good. Felt so good. I wanna do it again and again, forever."

Court made a strangled sound and looked into Lucan's eyes. "Forever?"

The word was like Court, cutting Lucan at the same time that it cradled him and kissed him. Maybe it was the comedown, but Lucan's eyes welled. "Yeah, babe. I'm yours."

Court's cum was hot on Lucan's stomach when it landed, some of it right over the cuts.

Court sighed deeply and fell onto his back on the floor. He gripped Lucan's hand and squeezed. "I'm sorry, but I love you."

Lucan swallowed thickly. "You're just saying that 'cause you're Top-high."

"Nope. I love you when I'm low, too."

Lucan didn't know how love felt anymore, couldn't remember it, but he didn't think he loved Court. Not yet. "Did I show you everything like you wanted?" he asked instead.

Court rolled his head to look at Lucan. "No. But we're getting there. You did a good job."

CHAPTER 12

LYING on the floor next to Lucan, sweaty and tired yet completely alert, Court was not okay. He didn't regret the *I love you*; that wasn't the problem. And it wasn't necessarily Lucan's reaction to it because Court wouldn't have expected anything more. But he was cut up inside, as if every slice he'd made on Lucan's stomach had had a mirror inside his skin.

Last time they'd had sex, Court had felt like this afterward. He'd thought it was just because he'd had painful thoughts during the scene. He'd remembered Lucan dumping him and had poured his pain into the fuck. But tonight, he'd been focused on one thing only: pleasuring Lucan. He'd gotten lost in Lucan's soft skin, his taste, his little whimpers and breaths and trembles and moans. Lucan had been obedient and sweet, and Court had come hard.

So why was this still painful?

"What is being Top-high supposed to feel like?" he asked. Lucan was the expert, right? Court had done some research lately; some websites mentioned Domspace or Topspace as the equivalent of subspace, but it seemed everybody cared much more about what bottoms experienced. He hadn't found any detailed accounts of what he should expect for himself in the aftermath.

"I don't know," Lucan answered. "I'm not a Top."

"I feel like you hurt me. Like I was the one under the knife." Maybe he shouldn't have shared that. Court was supposed to be caring for Lucan right now, giving him first aid and cuddles, but Lucan had said before that aftercare was for both of them. And they were holding hands, at least.

Lucan rolled onto his side and pressed a kiss to Court's shoulder. "Where does it hurt?"

Court rested his free hand over his chest. "Here."

"Hmm. Maybe you do love me."

A wash of anger flared in Court. "I told you I do."

"Shh. Just teasing." Where they were holding hands, Lucan pushed Court's palm against the cuts on his stomach. "I love these. Did you love giving them to me?"

Court smiled. Lucan had eaten up the pain, squirming and wanting to see what Court was writing so badly. "Yes. You were cute."

Lucan smiled, too, but wrinkled his nose. "'Cute'? Not drop-dead sexy?"

"Yes, cute. Adorable. You were charmed when I ate your ass, weren't you?"

Lucan laughed, goofy and loud, into Court's shoulder. The genuine sound took away some of the hurt in Court's chest.

"Yes, I was swept off my feet by that rimming. Literally." Lucan got on top of Court, straddling his hips. The eye contact he bestowed on him was unblinking and intense.

"What?" Court asked, heating despite having just come.

Lucan smiled. "I can't believe you're here."

"Well, I am." He ran his hands up Lucan's thighs and felt such a rush of affection that he had to say it again. "I love you."

"Are you trying to get me to say it back?" He asked it without malice.

"No."

"You're the only person I've ever loved, Court." The corners of his pretty mouth turned down. "How many people did you love since we broke up?"

Court thought about the guys he'd had. There was one, Tommy, whom he had seen for a few months, but they had never gotten to love. Just sex that left Court feeling unfulfilled.

"Nobody," he said.

Lucan gave a disbelieving sneer. "Really?"

"Yes, really."

"Lots of sex, though. So much that you and Cally have a *code*."

Court smirked. "That upsets you, huh? Should I have been celibate and pined for you instead?"

"Yep."

"Oh, shut up." Court gave Lucan a light swat on the hip.

Lucan laughed again, the sound more controlled this time. "Did you go for guys who looked like me?"

Court thought about it. Tommy had been a ginger. He tried to remember what his other hookups had looked like. Some of them had been blond, most of them slender but not all. "Not really. Maybe a little. I wasn't looking for your looks."

"What were you looking for?"

Did Court really need to say it? "Submission."

Lucan hummed and walked his fingers up Court's chest. "Are you telling me guys weren't begging to submit to you?"

Some had been like that, but as soon as Court had tried to spank them more than a few times, they'd protested. They hadn't gotten off on the idea of being bruised. On the other hand, Tommy had liked the bruises but not the submission. He'd wanted sex to be like a fight. He'd never gone soft, never let Court into his mind and heart.

"They weren't right," Court offered.

"Am I right?" Lucan wasn't looking at Court anymore.

"Of course. Why would you ask me that?"

"I feel inadequate."

"Luc, you're not—"

"No, shut up. I am inadequate. You said I hurt you. Well, it's 'cause I'm not reacting how you want. But like, you were the *only* one I loved. And it didn't work out, so I've been thinking love wasn't worth it, you know? And submitting like I submitted to you proved dangerous, so I thought, submitting is dangerous. Then every time I liked a guy, I'd be thinking over and over in the back of my head, 'Love isn't worth it, submission is dangerous. Love isn't worth it, submission is—'"

"Lucan."

Defiance hardened Lucan's features like he was silently daring Court to argue.

"I'm sorry it didn't work out," Court said, because he wasn't going to apologize for his actions anymore. He'd been young and ignorant and he'd fucked things up, but they'd talked about it already. "It *will* work out this time." He reached up and cupped Lucan's cheek. "I'll wait for you to get that. I've got all the time in the world."

Lucan's shoulders slumped a little, and he smiled dreamily. "Thanks."

This was the type of calmness Court liked to see on his submissive. "Did I say the right thing?"

"Yes, Alpha."

With a curled-up finger, Court brushed down the bridge of Lucan's nose. "Thank you for sharing your feelings with me."

Lucan settled back down on the floor and snuggled up to Court's side. "It can't be fun for you, though, me saying that stuff."

Court didn't know how to respond to that. "'Fun' isn't the right word, but..." He shrugged. "Honesty from you feels good. I worry about what you think about me when I'm not around. What you're feeling about us and not telling me." Court didn't want to go on, but it was only fair, right? Lucan had shared his fears. "I'm terrified you'll leave me again, and I won't be able to do anything about it. I *hate* feeling powerless. Hate it."

"A true Dom," said Lucan, and it sounded like a joke, and Court was really tempted to get up and walk away.

"Hey." With a warm hand on Court's cheek, Lucan brought him back. "I struggle with that because we both have to maintain the freedom to leave. It's unhealthy not to."

"I don't care." A rush of possessiveness had Court putting Lucan on his back again. He sunk between his legs and pressed flush against him. "Do you want to hear what I fantasize about sometimes? It'll freak you out." Heat licked Court's back and shoulders.

Lucan wrapped his arms around Court. "Tell me."

Court kissed the shell of Lucan's ear, then whispered right into it. "I think about tying you up, keeping you prisoner."

Lucan made a sound Court had never heard from him before: a twisted, utterly aroused, guttural moan. "That's so fucked-up, Court."

"Yeah, I'm fucked-up over you."

Lucan snaked a hand up the back of Court's neck and into his hair, rubbing his scalp. "What would you do if I ran?"

Oh, were they going there? Court's stomach turned inside out. "Catch you. Take you to bed. Fuck you hard to remind you who you belong to."

"This feels good, Alpha."

Court didn't know what Lucan meant. Was he in the fantasy, thinking about Court claiming him? Was he talking about now: Court pressed against him, pinning him to the floor? "What feels good, baby?"

"You in my head. Taking me to dark places with your words." Lucan made a soft sound and gripped Court's hair. "Go deeper. Hurt me with it. Please."

Court swallowed the nerves that tried to rise up. So what if he'd never done this type of thing before? No big deal. Lucan was into something, eyes closed, biting his lip, petting Court's bicep. He'd asked Court for more, and Court would deliver.

"I want to gag you." Court settled one hand over Lucan's mouth, and Lucan's eyes flew open, locking on Court's. His pupils were huge, and Court's stomach churned deliciously. "If you were my prisoner, I'd never let you talk. You'd have one of those rubber balls in your mouth, or a dildo gag, or my fucking cock 24/7."

Lucan's eyes closed halfway, eyelashes fluttering.

The urge to pinch Lucan's nose and cut off his air hit Court out of nowhere, but fuck, he wanted to do it so badly. Breath play... Was that on Lucan's limits list?

Court cleared his throat. "May I stop your breathing? Nod or shake your head."

Lucan melted, whimpering against Court's palm. Then he nodded.

Court's scalp tingled, and his chest felt...loose, full. No more pain.

He pinched Lucan's nose. At first, Lucan was still, but then his eyes flew wide open again, and he writhed under Court. Court knew he should let him breathe, but the power was too good. He had never been in such complete control over someone.

A beat later, he let go of Lucan's nose.

Lucan's nostrils flared as he fought to get air with Court's hand still over his mouth. Then he made noises like he was trying to speak.

Court was going to get scolded. He just knew it.

He removed his hand.

"Court, Court—" Lucan grappled at Court, pulling him that little bit closer, but they were already so close. Still, Lucan kept pulling, squeezing, like he was trying to put Court inside of him.

"What's wrong?" Court asked, high on Lucan's desperation but lost, floating in uncharted territory.

"I need you. Please. Fill me up, Court— Alpha. I'm sorry I keep saying the wrong name. Punish me for it if you want. Please, Court. I can't think. Please." The last word came out on a dry sob.

Court was drowning. Lucan was pulling him under somewhere he'd never been, but there was a voice—strong and uncompromising— that told Court he couldn't give Lucan what he wanted.

"We still haven't gotten tested like you said we needed to."

"Then get a condom! If you fucked all those guys, you must have one. Jesus Christ, we're not at *my* fucking house!" Lucan slapped Court on the shoulder as if to emphasize how much of an idiot he was, and Court had to agree. But Lucan's reactions were frying his brain; it wasn't his fault!

He shoved Lucan away and went to his nightstand's bottom drawer to get the condom. His hands shook as he put it on. When he looked up, Lucan was on his back on the bed, hand over his mouth, pinching his own nose.

Court had to laugh. In its way, that was just so adorable.

When Court crawled onto the bed, lube in hand, Lucan let himself breathe. After several deep intakes of air, he said, "It's better when you do it."

"I agree." Getting his cock into Lucan was a good idea, but Court hungered for the breath play more. He resumed his position on top of Lucan, hand over his mouth, thumb and pointer clamping his nostrils.

Again, it got truly erotic for Court when Lucan jerked for needing to breathe, and he held on longer than felt reasonable to drink in those last few jolts of Lucan's bones and muscles. When he let his nose go, he once more kept his hand in place so he could watch Lucan's nostrils flare, desperate for the oxygen.

Lucan moaned, as muffled as the sounds were, like he was getting the best fuck of his life—despite the fact that Court's dick was trapped against his lower stomach and nowhere near his hole.

Court uncovered Lucan's mouth and reached for the lube.

"I'm gonna get addicted again." Lucan's rambling, Court was beginning to realize, was a good sign. He hadn't done this during their sex in the past, but he'd been doing it a lot lately, and the words that came out were perfect to Court: honest, unfiltered, a gift.

Court lubed up his cock.

"I was addicted back then," said Lucan. "That's why I was such a piece of shit to you, why I pretended to want to fuck your friends."

"I know."

"If I get like that again, what will you do?" Helpfully, Lucan held up his bent legs, presenting his hole.

Court rubbed his cockhead there, wishing that latex barrier wasn't there to dull the sensations. "Flirt with some other guy, and I'll belt you so hard you'll beg me never to do it again."

Lucan's hole clenched as if desperate to be filled, and Court slapped it with his cock.

"I was almost Flame's."

Court forgot about his dick for a second. "What?"

"I did a few scenes with him, sucked his dick, but it just didn't work. I think he was too nice to me."

Imagining Flame's pretty face, gorgeous skin, and muscles at the helm of Lucan's pleasure made Court burn with jealousy. But Lucan liked that, didn't he? Or he wouldn't tell Court these things.

In one go, Court buried himself inside Lucan. It wasn't as smooth as it would have been if Court had stretched him with his fingers, but that was the point.

Lucan gave a strangled moan and wrapped his legs around Court.

"Does that ache, baby?" Court asked from under the glorious pressure cradling his dick.

"Mhm." Lucan petted and massaged Court wherever he could reach. "I stopped using my dildos. Wanna be tight for you."

Fuck. Court tried to remember what they'd been talking about before, but he couldn't make the fragments of it stick. It didn't matter, though. Lucan was under him, receptive and rambly and sweet, and Court didn't have anywhere to be but right here, eating it all up.

He set an easy pace, fucking Lucan at a steady rhythm until the energy around them calmed, and Lucan was watching Court, blinking slowly, making soft sounds whenever Court pushed deep into him.

"I'm sorry," Lucan was saying. "I'm sorry I was gone for so long, that I touched anybody else, that I didn't let you hurt me and love me and—"

"Shh." Court covered Lucan's mouth and nose again, envisioning himself as a wave taking Lucan under, stealing his breath. He let up, then did it again, let up, then did it again, over and over until Lucan's eyes wouldn't focus and his moans didn't stop unless Court made them.

Court felt truly as if he were on a cloud. The air around him buoyed him, took him and Lucan to another spiritual plane where pleasure was the only feeling that existed, and love couldn't be withheld because of things you'd said or hadn't done six years ago.

Time was bullshit; Court knew that now. Lucan had always been his.

Court pushed the limit of their play to a place that made him shiver. Lucan jerked particularly violently, and then his eyes snapped open, wide and fearful, and he grabbed and clawed at Court's hand and arm, digging burning scratches.

When Court let him go, Lucan gasped and arched.

Court fucked him as hard as he could. Lucan cried out with a rough voice and came between them, shooting and shooting much longer than anyone had ever done in Court's bed.

Court's head swam, and his cock was still achingly hard, squeezed inside Lucan's tight hole. He continued to pump his hips, chasing the climax that was just out of reach.

Lucan was limp and barely alert under him. His body rocked easily with the thrusts, his gaze just barely clinging to Court's face.

"Talk to me," Court demanded. "Touch me." *Look alive.*

Lucan lifted his hands to Court's face, the skin of them warm and slightly clammy. "Thank you." He pawed at his cheeks, traced his jawline, stroked down his throat. "Thank you."

The intimacy of the touches did wonderful things to Court's head, heart, and groin. As he pushed his body to its limit, thrusting and thrusting when he was way past tired, a droplet of sweat fell from his brow and dripped down his face.

Lucan caught it with the back of his hand. "You're mine, Court." He'd never said that before. Just *yours, I'm yours.* "If you ever do this shit with anyone else, I'll kill you. And that's not a figure of speech. I'll fucking do it. You're mine. *Mine.*" He scratched hard down the side of Court's neck, and Court came, riding the punches of pleasure with a gritty cry tearing from his throat.

Afterward, he had just enough energy to pull out, toss the condom away, and pull Lucan against him. "Stay."

Lucan scoffed. "Like I could walk right now."

Smiling so big it hurt his cheeks, Court gave Lucan's bare ass a tap.

CHAPTER 13

SPOTTY RAYS of sunlight from the distorted glass of the bathroom window played over Lucan's skin as he leaned against the sink. Court had a big first aid kit open on the closed toilet seat, and he was rifling through it collecting what he needed to treat Lucan's cuts from last night.

Lucan had a bizarre need to fight the aftercare as if he could prove in that way that Court was really serious about this.

"I can do it myself, honestly," said Lucan. "The cuts are super shallow. They probably don't even need a bandage."

"Shut your damn mouth," said Court.

Lucan grinned and clenched his fingers around the sink's hard edge, watching Court's half-naked, freshly showered form. His well-groomed, chestnut-colored hair swooped prettily, still damp.

Court tore open an alcohol swab and brought the glistening square to Lucan's stomach. It didn't hurt—just a tiny sting—but it was cool enough to make Lucan clench his stomach muscles. Next, Court squeezed a strip of ointment over the cuts and placed a rectangle of soft white gauze on top.

"Hold this," he said.

Lucan did.

Court secured the gauze with tape, running his fingers along the border of the bandage in a way that tickled. "There you go."

Lucan's stomach fluttered. "Thank you, Alpha." Elated, he pressed a hasty kiss to Court's face.

Court laughed. "I can see why people get so worked up about aftercare."

"Why?" Lucan knew his reasons, but he wanted to hear Court's.

Court shrugged. "Feels good. Like you're wrapped around me."

The description was simple, almost childlike, but Lucan understood; Court felt connected to him.

"I can be wrapped around you," Lucan teased.

Court pulled Lucan into a kiss. The way he licked into him, his tongue mint-tinged from his toothpaste, had a slight ache flaring in Lucan's hole. He loved being sore from a good fuck, and he'd take Court's cock again right this second if he wanted.

Too soon, Court pulled away. "Let's go out for breakfast."

Breakfast. "Are you saying"—Lucan put his hand to his chest in mock, touched surprise—"you want to take me somewhere that isn't a sex party or a bedroom?"

Court narrowed his eyes and tapped Lucan on the cheek. "What part of 'I love you' don't you understand?"

Lucan hooked a leg around the back of Court's thigh. "Are you going to get me flowers and shit now?"

"Maybe."

"A promise ring?"

Court laughed. "Isn't that for when you promise to stay a virgin? That ship has sailed."

"That's a *purity* ring."

"Well, I'm definitely not going to get you one of those." Court's face got serious again, and he traced a horizontal line across Lucan's throat. "Have you thought more about a collar?"

Lucan had, a little. And it made him uncomfortable—maybe because of how he'd be the only one wearing something. Why did he have to be marked in public while Court wasn't? He gave Court scratches, but they faded quickly, or they hid under his clothes.

"You don't want to," Court said, searching Lucan's gaze.

"I'd wear your collar. But I don't really like how most of them look. You can't wear them in the real world, or people will think you're some fetishy goth freak—"

"Then yours can be a necklace."

That might work. Lucan stroked Court's boxer-clad hip. "And you?"

Court frowned. "Me?"

"Would you hate wearing something for me? A—A bracelet? Or something?" He hadn't had this possessive urge for a long time, but it had hit him last night while his cock was softening and Court was trying to come. Court was his again—his Dominant, his boyfriend, his plaything—and all the pretty people at all the parties needed to know he was off-limits.

Court gave Lucan an unreadable look, though there was a slight upturn to his lips. "Okay," he said eventually.

"Do you not like the idea?"

"I like it fine."

"Then why are you looking at me so hard?" Lucan could feel Court thinking deeply about something. Why wasn't he sharing like he usually did?

But then he asked, "Do I need to worry about you flirting with people in front of me? Flame?"

Anxiety punched Lucan's stomach. Yes, Court needed to worry. Lucan shifted against the sink's hard ceramic. He knew it was wrong, that it hurt Court. But his jealous reaction was like a drug. When Lucan had mentioned Flame last night, Court's features had hardened, his gaze going dangerous, and he'd hurt Lucan by fucking him without prep.

It had only been a hint of how Court had punished him in the past. That thing with Ash, Court's frat brother, was what had torn them apart. Lucan had flirted with him shamelessly, and Court had punished him severely for it—more severely than he knew. The sex had been so good, but the drop had been terrible, and Lucan had sent Court the breakup text during it and ignored Court's responses. Later, he'd regretted the whole thing, and he'd texted Court, but Court hadn't answered. So Lucan had gone to the frat house. Its door had frequently been unlocked during the day, and Lucan had gone right in and to Court's closed bedroom door. He'd been about to knock, but then he'd heard the moans. And he'd heard Ash call out Court's name.

"Lucan!"

Lucan snapped back into the present. "What?"

"I asked you a question. Do I need to worry about you flirting with other guys to piss me off?"

Lucan did his best to shove the memory of Court's revenge sex back into the recesses of his mind where it belonged, but remnants remained like pieces of glass bobbing around inside him.

He cleared his throat. "Um. Is it a limit for you?"

"I don't know."

"And if I do it and you punish me, will you be mad at me afterward and not give me aftercare when I drop? Because that's why we broke up, and—"

"I don't know! Let me think about it."

The same day Lucan had heard Court and Ash together, Court had finally replied to Lucan's texts. He'd sent so many. *I love you*, and *I don't want to lose you*, and *Please answer me*, and variations of those and more. But Lucan had felt as if Court had torn out his heart and eaten it, so the texts hadn't touched him. He'd read them and deleted them—each and every one.

Court touched Lucan's cheek. "Hey. Where's your head at?"

Lucan gave a hollow laugh. "Nowhere good."

Court brushed Lucan's nose with his own. "Tell me, baby."

Lucan wanted to. Court was so close, so gentle. He ran his fingertips up Lucan's bare arm and looked at him with kind eyes.

But if Lucan talked about that terrible night right now, he'd spiral into a depression too deep to get out of—at least in time for breakfast.

"I'll tell you later. I'm hungry. Are we going to go eat?"

Court pursed his lips and stared at Lucan for several seconds before sighing. "Yes, we're going. Let's get dressed."

Lucan smiled and pecked Court on the cheek. "I'm thinking pancakes. What about you?"

* * *

Court had had a long day. He'd administered oxygen to a kid having an asthma attack, performed CPR on a man in cardiac arrest, and dealt with a heroin overdose. The OD had been the last call of the night, and Court couldn't shake the uncomfortable feeling in his gut about it even as his shift came to a close.

He had to admit, his job had a lot of similarities to Topspace. It didn't have the sexy bits, but it had the rush and the drop. Now came the drop.

In between the calls, Court had thought about Lucan's shitty jealousy kink. How he wanted to flirt with other guys to make Court punish him.

Court didn't get it. He could punish Lucan whenever; he didn't need to be pissed off for real to do that. But Lucan had said something about Flame the other night: *"He was too nice to me."*

Lucan harped about aftercare and answering texts and all that shit, but what he really wanted was abuse—then reassurance that everything was really fine between them.

The realization hit Court as he was digging his phone out of his locker. Several texts from Lucan were waiting for him. They'd just seen each other two days ago, and Court's resistance to reading the texts was an all-too-familiar feeling. But he pushed through it because the last thing he wanted was to hear Lucan accuse him of being a bad Dom again.

I know you're at work but I'm a mess

Will you answer as soon as you can? I feel off

Please, Court. I'm scared you're going to leave me because of how I am

I called into work. I've been thinking about your belt. Please

The last text had come less than an hour ago. Court tried to think clearly around the idea of belting Lucan, which was what he deserved. Should he go over there and do that for him? He could say it was a punishment for calling in to his job. EMTs didn't get to call in because they were having a bad day. Or, well, they could, but everyone would expect it to be a true emergency. An *I wasn't feeling up to it* wouldn't work.

Court swallowed hard before texting back. *Just finished my shift. Do I need to come over there and beat you?* Just using those taboo words had him breathing harder.

If it pleases you, Alpha. I know I deserve it

Court's stomach stirred, and he stuffed his phone into his pocket and made for his car at a near-run. He didn't need anybody he worked with to see him looking worked up.

In his car, he burned under the glow from his overhead light in the darkness. *Why do you think you deserve it, baby?*

Because I like making you jealous. And I know you don't like it. I know. You said you'd think about it, but you were just being nice

Court gritted his teeth. *Don't assume what you don't actually know. But you're right, it makes me sick.*

I love it when you're mad at me. When you hurt me when you're mad. But it's not safe kink. We're not supposed to lose control and I hate myself for this. I'm sorry, Alpha. I'm sorry

Court's fingers itched to grip the stiff leather of his belt and wail on Lucan until welts sprung up on him.

I'm coming over.

Thank you, Alpha

You won't be thanking me when I get there. You'll be begging me to stop, but I won't.

Because I'm a slut, Alpha?

I won't argue with that, but no. Because I'm pissed off.

* * *

Court ascended the front steps of Lucan's house, his blood sizzling in his veins. Before he even knocked, the door opened, and Lucan's scared face appeared.

Court stormed inside, pushing Lucan back. But then he noticed the projector screen flickering on the wall of the otherwise dark living room and Lucan's roommates on the couch.

"You know the traffic light safewords?" Lucan asked. "I forgot to go over them. Red for stop, yellow for slow down, green for—"

"Keep going," Court finished. "Yeah."

Dom was staring at them, gaze full of cold judgment, his dark eyes like glass in the projector's light. What did Dom think of this? Could he sense what Court was about to do? Being kinky, any of these people could probably tell that Lucan was terrified, and what would that mean but an impending punishment?

Well, Lucan *should* be terrified.

Lowly, Court said, "Get your ass upstairs." Then he nudged Lucan forward.

As they finally got moving, it seemed Lucan was walking slowly on purpose. God, Court was going to murder him!

Lucan's room was brightly lit. As soon as they'd crossed the threshold, Court went for his belt.

"Wait!" Lucan's hands were hot on Court's arms, stopping him.

"For what?" Court nearly yelled.

"No sex."

"Excuse me?"

"No sex, Court! Just beat me. Please!"

Court wished—for *once*—that he could truly be the one in control here. But Lucan always had a goddamn stipulation. He was always holding him back!

Court undid his belt buckle. "Is this because you're hell-bent on making sure I'm not diseased? Even though I *know* I'm not?"

Lucan grew a shell, standing straighter and crossing his arms. "How am I supposed to believe you're Mr. Safe Sex, huh? You hate condoms!"

Court's frustration with Lucan built to a dangerous level. "Maybe if every time I talked to you I didn't fall immediately into your fucking web of drama, we'd have made an appointment already!"

Lucan scoffed. "My *web* of *drama*? Fuck you!"

Court had had enough. All right—he wouldn't have sex with Lucan tonight. He wouldn't touch his dick at all, in fact. But he *was* going to cover him in nasty red stripes, and he was going to start right now.

He gripped Lucan by the T-shirt and threw him at the bed. Lucan tried and failed to right himself, but Court saved him from the responsibility, yanking and pushing until he had him bent over the foot of the bed. He pulled down Lucan's pants and underwear, leaving them in a pile at his ankles.

"This is what you want, isn't it?" Court asked. Because while his desire to hit Lucan was still overwhelming, uncertainty was blooming in his chest like an ugly plant that wouldn't die. "You want me to hit you until I'm satisfied but leave that pretty dick and pussy alone?"

Lucan looked over his shoulder, gaze intense. "Yes, Alpha. Green."

Court slid his belt out of the loops on his work uniform and folded it, gripping the ends. Lucan was still watching, eyes flicking from the belt to Court's face.

"You're going to tell me thank you after every hit. Is that clear?" Court asked.

"Yes, Alpha."

Court started. When the leather connected with Lucan's ass for the first time, Court exhaled, his cock twitched, and a weight came off his shoulders.

This felt right—just like Lucan calling him Alpha, waking up with Lucan next to him, slicing his name into Lucan's stomach, and kissing Lucan hello and goodbye.

"Thank you," said Lucan.

Court's belt was much more effective than his hand at turning the skin red. Just a few hits accomplished that, and as he kept going, welts formed in the shape of his belt from one side of Lucan's ass to the other.

Lucan's thank-yous grew quieter, and he sniffled. Court examined Lucan's ass, touching the skin lightly. Whenever his fingertips connected with the inflamed flesh, Lucan tensed, and Court weathered simultaneous rushes of satisfaction and sympathy. Court knew how far he could go and be able to care for the injuries himself, but was Lucan enjoying this?

Court gripped Lucan's hair and tilted his head back. Tears made Lucan's cheeks glisten.

"More?" Court asked.

"Green," said Lucan.

Court resumed the hits. Lucan's thank-yous became music to him, and though his cock was hard, bodily arousal became secondary to the physical and emotional act of having Lucan submit like this. Across the middle of Court's fleshy canvas, the skin became tinged dark red, then purple, and Lucan was screaming his thank-yous and shaking with sobs.

Court gave Lucan a last hard whack before dropping the belt.

The welts and forming bruises were hot to the touch. Lucan didn't squirm anymore, just sobbed, his arms curled around him, his back bowed, and half his face buried in his messy bedsheets.

Court ran gentle hands down Lucan's back, soothing and loving. He would have liked to gather Lucan up and make love to him, which was why Court would make damn sure they went to a walk-in testing clinic together as soon as they could. He knew of multiple places they could go. He also knew Pittsburgh had a high STI rate, but he'd been dragging his feet on this for the reason he'd given Lucan—he kept getting too wrapped up in all the kinky stuff he wanted to do to him.

For Lucan's aftercare, Court dropped into emergency response mode. If he responded to a call and found someone all bruised up and welted, he'd ice the wounds and advise them to take acetaminophen.

"Is it okay if I raid your kitchen for something to ice you with?" he asked.

"Yes, Alpha."

"And where do you keep your painkillers?"

"Bathroom."

Court bent to give Lucan a kiss between the shoulder blades. "I'll be right back. I love you."

"Love you, too, Alpha."

The words made Court freeze. Had Lucan really said them? "You love me?" he blurted. Lucan was probably just endorphin-high and feeling extra grateful for the rough treatment he hadn't been able to get from Flame or Dom.

Lucan pushed himself up, and Court grabbed him, helping him stand and step out of the clothes around his ankles. He was adorable with just his T-shirt on, eyes puffy, hair a mess.

He wrapped his arms around Court's neck and pressed their foreheads together. "Yeah, I think I do love you. I don't really know how it's supposed to feel. Is that stupid?"

"No."

"I'm a shitty teacher. I get too lost. I let things slide. Thank you for not fucking me when I asked you not to."

Court held Lucan's face and made him look him in the eye. "Do you think I would ignore that?"

Lucan shrugged, winced. "I still would have liked it! I like everything you do. Rules stop mattering to me when you touch me. I shouldn't be telling you this. I'm a bad teacher. You'll get the wrong idea…" Lucan started breathing too quickly.

"Baby." An idea struck Court. Oddly, he felt more mentally acute after belting Lucan than at any other time. "I want you to do something for me. I want you to write down everything you're worried about when it comes to us. Then we can address them one by one, and we won't forget."

Lucan nodded. "Okay."

"And I want your work schedule for as long as you have it. I'll pick you up, and we'll go to the clinic. That'll be the first worry we take care of."

Fresh tears spilled from Lucan's eyes. "Thank you, Alpha." He hugged Court like a scared kid or grateful parent at the scene of an emergency.

Court rubbed his back. "Everything is going to be okay." He felt elated, high, perfect. He needed to punish Lucan more often. It made things better, brought them closer, made Lucan surrender to Court's judgment, which was not as flawed as Lucan thought. Court was a good Dom—a *good* Dom!

He pulled out of the hug. "Lie down on your side, please. I'm going to go hunt down some ice."

Lucan kissed Court on the cheek before doing as told.

In the kitchen, Court was emptying multiple ice trays into a resealable bag when he ran into Dom.

"Sorry," said Court. "I'll refill them, but I need the ice for Lucan."

Dom's confident, unforgiving gaze made Court uncomfortable, but he ignored the feeling.

"What did you do to him?" Dom asked.

"Belt," Court offered curtly.

"We all heard him scream."

For some reason, the words dug into Court like barbs. Why did Dom feel the need to tell Court this? How was what Court did to Lucan Dom's business anyway? "Next time, I'll gag him. I wasn't worried about it at the time."

Dom chuckled. "Guys like you don't worry about anything."

Court sealed the bag of ice and set it on the hand towel he'd grabbed. "Do you have a problem with me?" He met Dom's eyes unflinchingly.

Dom smiled, though it was hardly friendly. "Just looking out for my friend. Others in the community would be much better for him. This teaching thing..." Dom made a vague, circular gesture. "It won't work. Lucan goes into subspace too easily. He can't keep an eye on you."

Court saw red, but on the outside, he appeared as put together as ever. "Maybe we should invite *you* to keep an eye on me. You could watch me fuck him."

Dom laughed. "That's really not what I meant."

"Would you like to watch me suffocate him? He gets off on that. *Really* gets off. That"—Court mirrored Dom's vague gesture from earlier—"feather shit you do doesn't hold up." Court wasn't all that familiar with sensation play, but he knew enough about it from browsing FetNet—and from creeping on Dom's profile. It was fine for some people, but not for Lucan.

Dom smiled again. Anger and fierce dislike radiated off him. "You'd better get going. Your ice is going to melt."

"You're right. Thank you." Court snatched the ice and towel off the counter and headed for the bathroom to look for painkillers. Dom had left a bitter taste in his mouth, but once he was with Lucan again, icing his welts and feeding him Tylenol, nothing else mattered.

CHAPTER 14

As they drove away from the testing clinic, Lucan intertwined his fingers with Court's where they rested their hands on the center console. It was a weight off his shoulders to have Court tested for STIs, even if they had to wait a few days for some of the results. What they'd been able to hear about today had been good—all negative.

Lucan had expected that they probably wouldn't test positive for something—at least, *he* wouldn't—but with Court wanting to throw his cum everywhere while Lucan was in subspace, it was just better to know for sure.

Plus, as soon as they got the blood work back and everything was fine, Lucan would get to feel Court come in him, completely worry-free...

"You said you know a place with collars?" Court asked.

Lucan blinked. "Uh, right. It's in Lawrenceville. By that bikes shop."

"What's it called?"

"The Fetish Palace."

Court gave Lucan a sideways glance.

Lucan smirked. "It's a newer place. A little small for a palace, but it has a lot of cool stuff. Like twenty-five percent of my toys came from there."

"Only twenty-five percent?"

Lucan shrugged. "I'm picky. I order most of them online." When he could afford them, anyway. Fetish gear wasn't cheap, and Lucan didn't make that much as a waiter. Mainly just enough to pay his bills, buy food, and afford the cover charges at parties. He had a little money to afford whatever he could get Court to wear for him. Hopefully. Would Court expect to pay for Lucan's collar?

"You're tensing up," said Court, and Lucan realized he was squeezing Court's hand a little too tightly.

He pulled away and reached for his phone. "Just thinking about how much collars cost."

"Don't worry about it. I'll buy what we need."

Lucan gave Court a look. "EMTs don't make that much."

"I make enough for this. It's important. Speaking of..." Court stopped at a red light and focused on Lucan. "Did you bring the list?"

Oh no—the list.

"What list?" Lucan asked casually.

"Don't play dumb with me."

Court had told Lucan last night to bring his list of worries—the one that had sounded so good when he'd been in subspace last week but which made his skin crawl now. He hadn't liked writing it, either, or folding it into a little square and putting it into his back pocket. But Lucan understood why Court had had him make it, and he even admired the order—cherished it—deep down.

"Of course I brought it," said Lucan.

"Use that tone with me again," Court warned.

The interior of the car got stuffy suddenly. "Sorry, Alpha. Yes, I brought it."

"Let's stop somewhere and go over it before we look at collars."

Lucan coughed. Was Court serious? "You want to talk about my deepest fears in public?"

Court was quiet for a second, and his jaw clenched visibly, jumping under his clean-shaven skin. "Yeah, I don't think it will be a big deal. We'll find a corner."

Lucan groaned and covered his face with his arms.

Court rubbed Lucan's shoulder. "Don't be dramatic, baby. I'll buy you whatever you want. A muffin, a delicious, sugary beverage..."

"Mr. Moneybags," Lucan grumbled.

"Is bribery a limit for you?"

Outwardly, Lucan continued to sulk, but he also imagined a blended coffee with lots of whipped cream and chocolate syrup. "No, Alpha."

* * *

Lucan sipped at his blended coffee and looked anywhere but at Court. In the cafe they'd chosen, Court had indeed found them a somewhat secluded corner. Though Lucan wouldn't look at him, he could tell by the utter serenity coming from across the small table that Court was in his element and not nervous about this at all. Did he think the things on Lucan's list would be trivial?

"All right, let's see it." Court set down his mug, the ceramic thudding against the table like a gavel.

Lucan knew if he tried to stall any longer, he'd just make Court mad. And he'd have to suffer through this eventually.

He reached into his back pocket and produced the folded-up list.

Carefully, Court unfolded it. From his pocket, he pulled a pen. "Okay. Number one."

Lucan focused hard on the milky, chocolatey goodness that was his blended coffee.

"Court will give me an STI," Court read aloud. "Well, we can cross that one out." And he did. "Number two. 'Court will get overwhelmed by how much I want him to dominate me.'"

A dreadful heat engulfed Lucan's whole face.

"Look at me, babe."

Lucan did.

Court's gaze was soft, pretty. "Everything's going to be okay, all right? We're just talking. Nothing terrible will happen because of your worries."

"You don't know that."

Court's mouth tightened. "I'll read ahead and let you know."

"No!" Without thinking, Lucan snatched the list from Court's side of the table.

Court's fist came down onto the table's chrome surface, but it wasn't a hard hit; it barely made a sound. "You're lucky we're in public."

"I—I just—" Lucan folded the list from the bottom so that all the items were covered except for one and two. "Please, just one at a time." Nervously, he slid the list back toward Court.

Court gave him a stony look, but then he sighed, refocusing on the task. "I get why you're worried about me being overwhelmed. I ignored you in college a few times when I was stressed about school."

"Yeah," said Lucan, the memories of wanting to see Court so badly biting at him. "Sometimes, when you weren't around, I ached for you. I think it was sub drop. But I'd want you so bad, and you wouldn't answer me, and I'd be just short of showing up at the frat house. A couple times, I actually did, but you weren't there. I was so needy and powerless."

Court rested his hand palm up on the table, and Lucan slid his on top.

"I'm sorry," Court said. "I've gotten overwhelmed a couple times lately."

Lucan snapped his gaze up, squeezed Court's wrist. Fear cut through him, but he tried really hard to look calm. "You have?"

"Yes. I didn't ignore you, though."

Lucan knew he was going to sound crazy saying it, but he couldn't stop himself. "Well, there was that time we didn't see each other for like two weeks. I wondered..."

Court chewed on his lip and didn't say anything for far too many seconds.

"Maybe *you* should make a fucking worry list," said Lucan.

"Hey." Court gave Lucan's arm a tug. "Don't snap off at me. I'm going to explain."

"Explain faster."

"Remember who you're talking to." Court dug his thumb nail into the underside of Lucan's arm until it stung, and he didn't let up. "I'm your Dom. I take care of you. We work through our problems, which is what we're doing right now. You can take it, baby, and you can do it without treating me like shit. Isn't that right, Lucan?"

Court's control fell over Lucan like a gentle cage. The little bite of pain helped ground him, though any more and he'd get too aroused to talk about their problems.

"Yes, Alpha," he said.

"Good boy." Court removed his thumbnail, which left a red half-moon in its wake, and then bent over the table and kissed it.

Lucan glanced around the cafe. No one was watching them.

Court sat up straight. "So those couple of weeks. I was feeling out of sorts, and I should have told you. I realized after I made you cry during sex that I resented you for dumping me, that it still hurt even though it's been years. I needed a little time."

Lucan didn't know what to say. "Okay."

"But I didn't ignore you."

Did Court want a gold star for that? "Yeah, but I could feel something was off, and I don't want you to talk to me if you don't want to talk to me. I mean, how's that a good time for either of us?"

Court narrowed his eyes. "Then what do you want me to do?"

"I don't know!" Lucan stopped touching Court and took a sip of his blended coffee. "Tell me you're feeling overwhelmed and you'll talk to me later? But that you still love me? And then tell me what's going on in your head eventually because that's kind of important, you fucking *resenting* me." *Do you still resent me?* Lucan wrapped his arms around himself.

"I can do that."

"Okay." Lucan wanted to tell Court that he'd regretted dumping him and wanted to take it back—so there was no reason for him to be mad at Lucan! But that would come up later in the list.

The list's paper crinkled softly as Court picked it back up. "I'm not overwhelmed by your urge to be dominated, though. Just saying."

Lucan flushed—pleasantly this time. "Okay."

Court crossed out number two. Then he modified Lucan's fold to show the third list item. "Number three. 'Court will ignore me when I'm having sub drop.' Well, I'm not going to do that, so..." He crossed it out. "Number four. 'Court will be unavailable because of something outside of his control when I'm having sub drop, and in my irrational state, I'll blame him and he'll think I'm crazy and/or get pissed off.'" Court exhaled and looked up. "Don't worry about this one. I can take it."

Under the table, Lucan wiggled his toes in his shoes. "If you say so."

"I do say so."

Lucan should think of something more to say, to stall the next item—

"Number five."

Lucan winced in anticipation.

"I'll get antsy for Court's attention and be bratty and/or flirt with somebody else and he won't like it. He'll reject me. He'll dump me." Court took a breath.

Lucan laughed. "This is the part where I start wanting to die."

Court set the list down and tapped it with two fingers. "I don't understand this."

Lucan shrugged and became very interested in a piece of ugly abstract art on the wall.

"If you feel needy for me, just say so, Lucan. You don't need to hurt my feelings to get me to fuck you."

"That isn't—" Lucan pinched the bridge of his nose. Why did Court have to make him out to be such an asshole? "It's not about hurting your feelings."

"Too bad. Because that's what happens when you flirt with other people. And being bratty? Fuck that. Just submit—"

"Maybe sometimes I crave it rough."

Court squinted. "I don't do it rough enough for you?"

"I love how you dominate me. But sometimes..." Lucan's stomach churned. He shouldn't say this, shouldn't want it. He should bury this desire and stop voicing it because it would only confuse Court. Lucan never should have agreed to be his teacher. "I want you to hit me like you hate me. Put me in my place." Lucan was on fire again, and he didn't know if it was good heat or bad. "I mean, I still need it safe. It has to be *safe*—no permanent injuries. But that anger is what makes it perfect. And if I flirt..." Court was staring at Lucan like he'd gone completely off his rocker, but Lucan went on. He'd said so much, he might as well get it all out. "If I flirt, there's that claiming element to it. Like you hate me, but I'm still yours, and you won't give me up even when I'm bad." Lucan took a shaky breath. "Tell me you get it."

Court stared at Lucan for a few more seconds. "I get it, but that anger comes from pain. It hurts me that you would even make yourself *look* available to another guy."

Lucan knew he was a hypocrite. He wanted Court to respect his limits, but he didn't want to respect Court's. Except he *did*, and this was obviously a limit for Court, even if he hadn't worded it like that. "I know. I won't do it, okay? I won't do it."

"You want to, though."

"So? It's not worth—not worth losing you. Or making you hate me." He stared at that ugly painting again: blue and green and red swirls. The colors were jarring together.

"Bratty is when you don't submit, right?" Court asked.

And Lucan felt like even more of an asshole, because he shouldn't have even put that into number five. It conflicted with Court's must-have of submission. "It means putting up a fight. Submission comes eventually." Well, it was the truth. Bratty subs were still subs. But Court obviously didn't like that shit, either. "We don't need to—"

"We can try that. If it doesn't involve making me jealous."

Lucan licked his lips. "Yeah? You sure?"

"I don't think I really understand it, but we can try it. Just once to see."

It felt like they'd weathered a storm that was now clearing. "Okay. Thank you, Alpha."

But now came the last thing on Lucan's list, and it was a big one. An awful one.

Court unfolded the list all the way. "Number six. 'Court will have sex with someone else.'"

Lucan picked at the skin around his nails until blood sprouted at the base of one.

"That's rich, honestly," said Court. "You wanna flirt with people—"

"*Flirt*. Not fuck."

Court smiled, hummed, looked away. He tapped the table with his knuckles. "Why in the hell would you ever think I would cheat on you?"

Lucan had to say it now, didn't he? What he hadn't said the last time they'd lain together, and memories of their breakup had cut him inside his head. "After I broke up with you..."

Court watched him expectantly, and Lucan's mouth went dry.

He took another sip of his drink. "After I broke up with you, I tried to take it back. I went to the frat house to tell you, but you were..." Lucan's eyes welled, and he wished he wasn't here, doing this, feeling this. Was being Court's submissive again really worth reliving the moments when he'd felt smallest? "You were fucking Ash. I–I heard you."

Court's face slackened, his eyes widening in surprise. "What?"

"Yeah." Lucan sniffed and wiped at his eyes. "I know we were broken up, but like...it ruined me. That you would go to someone else so quickly. It fucked me up, and I couldn't talk to you."

Court was still looking at him with that stupid expression on his face, and Lucan couldn't stand it. He couldn't stand *Court*; he couldn't deal with any of this! "So yeah, resent me for *that*, Alpha. 'Cause I resent the fuck out of you."

Court pressed his lips together and nodded. Eventually, he stood. "I'm going to go buy myself a lemon square or something. You want anything else?"

Lucan gripped the chilly, condensation-soaked cup that still held half a blended coffee. "No."

Court ruffled Lucan's hair as he passed him, and Lucan roughly put the strands back where they belonged.

CHAPTER 15

COURT HAD EATEN ALMOST all of his lemon square and still hadn't said a word. But it was just that he wasn't sure how to explain this. Would Lucan even understand? He obviously felt like he'd been cheated on, which *wasn't* the case. Lucan had dumped Court, Court had done some shots with Ash, and then Court's dick had ended up smashed against Ash's because that had been the only way he could feel better.

He'd thought he'd lost his boy forever. Lucan had said that hearing Court fuck Ash had crushed him, well... Court didn't know a better word than *crushed* for how he'd felt after Lucan had told him they were over.

"Aren't you going to say something?" Lucan asked. He wasn't crying anymore, though he was trembling and had his arms wrapped around himself. Court suspected it was because he'd downed the rest of his blended coffee in like one second and was now cold.

Court ate the last bite of his lemon square and licked the tips of his fingers. "Are you going to be satisfied if I tell you it didn't mean anything? Because it didn't. I was wasted, Ash was a safe person to have a sad fuck with, and it wouldn't have happened at all if you hadn't dumped me. And that's the truth." Court didn't want to be mean, but he also didn't want to be the bad guy in another memory because he didn't deserve it—not this time.

Lucan scowled and looked away, showing Court his well-formed profile. "I don't know. What if the situation were reversed?"

Court considered that—and what an apt fucking question for everything they were going through. How would Lucan feel if Court had dumped *him* in an emotional moment? What if *Court* had wanted to take it back a few days later like Lucan was just some toy he could fuck with? What if when they saw each other years after the fact, Lucan was still hung up, and Court acted like he didn't want anything to do with him because everything had been obviously Lucan's fault?

The new perspective was like a match hitting gasoline.

"I would never have dumped you on a whim like that." Court's voice came out gravelly and cruel, and he liked how it felt scraping the back of his throat. "You deserved to hear me fuck Ash after how you treated me."

Lucan gasped. "Fuck you!"

The exclamation turned a few gazes onto them, and Court stood and straightened his button-down—he'd wanted to look nice on this special day of buying a collar—before snapping his fingers and pointing toward the door. "Go to the car. Let's not cause a scene."

Surprisingly, Lucan obeyed. Court gathered his plate and Lucan's empty cup and put them in the appropriate places before heading out as well.

Lucan was standing by the car with his arms crossed, all-out crying.

Court did not feel sorry for him in this instance. Especially not when he got closer and Lucan pushed him.

Court could not do what he wanted in broad daylight: shove Lucan against the car, grip his jaw, ask him who the fuck did he think he was in the presence of—Dom? Flame? So instead, he ignored Lucan's violent disobedience and got into the car.

Lucan did not follow Court's lead.

Court turned on the car and rolled down the window. "Get in."

"No." Lucan was doing something on his phone now. "I'll have someone come get me."

"The hell you will. Get in the fucking car. We are not done talking about this."

"No!" Lucan's eyes blazed when he looked up. "That shit hurt me so bad, and you say I deserved it! You don't love me. If you loved me, you wouldn't say shit like that."

Oh, please. Court could feel the ice coming down over him. His heart hardened, and he was suddenly completely fine with leaving Lucan here to get a ride from someone. But not yet.

"You didn't love *me* back then if you could give me up so easily."

Lucan gave a guttural shout. "I wasn't going to give you up! I was coming to fucking fix things!"

"Well, I'm sorry I couldn't cope with losing the love of my life in a way you approved of!"

Lucan smiled painfully and looked away. "The love of your life, huh?" He chuckled. "Am I still that? You still want to put a collar on me?"

The idea of a symbol of ownership around Lucan's neck still appealed, but this wasn't how Court wanted to feel when he made that happen. If he was going to be with Lucan again, it would be for real— and forever. This feeling like they were constantly hanging by a thread, just seconds from breaking into a disagreement that could break them up... He was over it. And he was over feeling like shit almost every time he saw Lucan.

This wasn't the time to put that collar around Lucan's neck; Court got that now.

"Maybe later," he said.

"Maybe later," Lucan echoed hopelessly, the sagging lines of his shoulders pointing to despair.

Court wasn't completely hardened; distantly, he felt for him. But this was too much. It was just too much.

Lucan checked his phone. "Flame's coming to get me."

The words hit Court like tiny spears, chipping away at the ice around his heart and nicking the tender flesh underneath. When would Lucan stop finding ways to hurt him?

"Are you fucking kidding me?" Court wanted to sound angry but could only manage a flat tone. "Not Dom or Roland?"

"They didn't answer, Court! I don't have that many friends."

"Maybe there's a reason for that."

Lucan's face twisted with sadness, his lips parting and his brows drooping.

Court rolled up his window. He'd reached his limit here because nothing good could come from staying any longer. He didn't have any kind words for Lucan, and apparently, Lucan had only cruel ones for him.

Once he had driven out of Lucan's sight, Court shouted out his pain to the interior of his car. Afterward, his throat hurt, and he felt like an idiot. His mind ran with thoughts of Lucan, turning over bits of their conversation and feeling the pain of them again. How could Lucan have suggested that Court would *ever* have acted like Lucan did in the past? Yeah, he'd been naïve about their kink. He hadn't provided Lucan with adequate aftercare, and he'd been distant sometimes, but giving up on them completely? That had been Lucan's doing. He hadn't communicated, so Court had had no way of knowing how to prevent sub drop. And he hadn't realized he'd needed to do *research* to have rough sex. That's all he'd thought their play was back then—rough sex like he'd seen in porn.

A sickness welled in his stomach and kept growing. He was losing Lucan again, wasn't he? And he wasn't sure he had the motivation to beg him back. If it was just going to be more of this—more blame, resentment, resistance, tears—what was the point? Trying to go backward hadn't given him or Lucan anything so far except a few instances of great sex and a whole lot of anguish. Court should do what he'd planned to do in the beginning: start new with someone else.

The idea of that had him crying actual tears. When he caught his reflection in the rear-view mirror, he winced and wiped away the moisture.

This was bullshit. He didn't deserve to feel this way. He wished he'd never met Lucan!

* * *

Flame showed up in the cafe's parking lot with open arms—literally.

Despite the fact that Lucan was still a crybaby mess and would have liked to snuggle up to Flame's muscular torso, he declined the offer for a hug and climbed into the passenger's seat of Flame's red truck. Even though he was furious at Court and aching from his cruel words, it still felt like betrayal to touch somebody else—platonically or not.

Once he was back at the wheel, Flame asked, "We going somewhere, or you want to go home?"

Lucan scoffed. "Do I look like I'm in any shape to go anywhere?" He caught his reflection in the truck's side mirror. His whole face was puffy and red; he looked *terrible*.

"You look like you might need a distraction," said Flame.

"I'm an emotional sadist's wet dream right now, and you know it."

Flame laughed, the sound musical and confident. That confidence had been what had drawn Lucan to him when they'd made a go at dating about a year ago. He wished it still appealed. He wished he'd been able to get into the things they'd done together, which had been exactly what he'd asked for. A few good spankings, one instance of rough head. And it had all been done with the utmost attention to aftercare and Lucan's well-being.

Lucan was beginning to think there was something wrong with him. He kept trying to get Court to be the perfect Dom like Flame seemed to be, but Lucan needed that element of cruelty to be satisfied. And Court had it, but it was where that shitty comment about Lucan deserving to hear him with Ash had come from. Lucan couldn't stomach cruelty at this level. He needed to know Court didn't want him in this type of pain, but he did. Or he wouldn't have said that.

"Home it is," said Flame gently. Lucan had to give him the address because they'd only met up at parties and played publicly together in the past.

Really, Lucan shouldn't have called him. But he hadn't been lying when he'd said no one else had answered. Dom and Roland were both at work, and Erin shared a car with Roland.

As they got out onto the road, the sunlight beaming into the truck was painfully at odds with Lucan's stormy insides.

"I know you're hurting right now, but I gotta say something," said Flame.

God. What could this be? "Okay," said Lucan warily.

"Dom came to me about you."

If he'd had the energy, Lucan would have laughed. "You're kidding."

"No, he said Court is dangerous for you, doesn't treat you right. Thought we should intervene."

Lucan clamped his eyes shut. What in the fuck? Why would Dom not come to Lucan if he had concerns?

"I told him to back off," said Flame.

"Thanks."

"Do you want to know why?"

Lucan sighed hard against the window. "Why?"

"Because you need someone who can keep you in turmoil and bring your body to the edge. I don't know much about Court, but from Dom's description, he seems like the guy."

What a sentence. Keep Lucan in turmoil? Dom's description?

"And just what the fuck did Dom tell you?"

"Hey now—"

"Don't fucking scold me. I've had about enough of being scolded when I'm not in the fucking wrong. *You* knew I was upset when you decided to divulge this bullshit."

Flame ran his tongue over his teeth. "Man, you're lucky you aren't mine. I'd make you eat soap for all those bad words."

"Just tell me what he said, Flame."

Flame gave him a stern look but eventually continued. "He said you didn't like private play, but you were doing all sorts of it with Court and that it was really violent. Everybody in the house heard you scream—"

"Oh, fantastic."

"—and this is a quote, 'That's about all they hear from you these days. It can't be healthy.'"

"Who's saying it's not healthy? Dom or you?"

"Dom."

"Well, it's really none of his fucking business. He's just jealous."

"That's basically what I told him. And that you have a different relationship with Court, so it's a different dynamic."

Lucan didn't want to think about his and Court's *dynamic* right now. But it was inevitable. "None of it matters because Court and I aren't going to last. We might already be over." Saying it out loud made Lucan feel hollow, like Court had surgically opened him up and removed all his organs.

"What happened today?" Flame asked. "What did you guys fight about?"

"You don't want to hear it."

"I asked, didn't I?"

Feeling numb, Lucan launched into an explanation of the worry list and how it had been a productive situation until Lucan's last worry about Court cheating.

"You flat-out told him you don't trust him to be faithful to you. Do you have a reason for that?" Flame asked.

Lucan told the story of catching Court with Ash, how painful it had been, what Court had said to Lucan in the cafe. That was when things got really uncomfortable in the truck, and though they were getting closer to Lucan's house, traffic was shit since it was still around lunchtime on a weekday.

"Did Court really call you the love of his life?" Flame's usually smooth face was scrunched into a pained wince.

"Yeah," said Lucan.

"You have *got* to cut him some slack with what he did. He was in pain."

Leave it to Flame to take Court's side.

"He won't cut *me* any slack," said Lucan. "He hates me for dumping him, but I had really bad sub drop, and I didn't know what was happening. I just knew I was hurting because of what he'd done to me."

Flame pressed his lips together and shook his head. "You've both got to let this shit go. Plenty of people try kink when they're inexperienced and fuck it up. That's what happened, and it's okay."

The words touched Lucan in a tender place, and he frowned and shifted in his seat. "You should tell Court that."

"Maybe I will."

"No, don't. He's so jealous of you."

Flame smirked. "I bet you rub it in his face, don't you?"

Lucan didn't answer.

"Yeah, I know you do. You love that shit."

* * *

At Lucan's place, Lucan gave Flame a kiss on the cheek and thanked him for the ride and the talk. Once Flame was gone, Lucan wished he'd asked him to stay. The house was empty and painfully quiet, leaving too much room for the reality of his situation.

He went straight to his bedroom, stripped to his boxers, and got into bed. His skin hurt. His phone didn't have any notifications.

What was Court doing right now? Was he in pain, too? Was he browsing FetNet, sending dick pics to people, looking for a lay? The tactic rarely worked on people, but Court had that nice dick with that pretty piercing.

Lucan didn't really believe that Court would go after someone else right now—they hadn't broken up, right? But the worry still lingered.

Lucan traced the faint lines left on his stomach where Court had cut him. He relived Court's gentle fingers bandaging him up. He wanted bandaged now, wanted Court's arms around him, wanted one of those delicious pecks on the forehead.

He would have taken more cuts, too, more lashes from Court's belt.

It was probably too soon to text Court. They both needed space to process things, right? Court hadn't had Flame's wise words to bring him a new perspective and was probably still wallowing in all the shitty things they'd said to each other.

But Lucan would be stuck here in this hole of sadness until he talked to Court. His Alpha was the only thing that would fix this, and why did Court need to wallow if they could talk instead?

Lucan opened a new text to Court, but he didn't know what to say. What if he didn't answer? What would *make* him answer?

Deciding to start simple, he said, *I'm sorry for not understanding that you were in a lot of pain when you went to Ash*

Court answered immediately, and hope surged into Lucan's chest.

It's cool. I mean, why start worrying about my feelings now? You don't give a shit about me. You just want to get high.

Lucan deflated. How could Court put that on him when their whole relationship centered around kink? Reaching oblivion together was the point, but that didn't mean Lucan didn't care. He wanted them both to be happy.

I like getting high with you. And I do care about you and your feelings. Can you understand mine back then? I was in a lot of pain when I broke up with you. I didn't understand subspace and sub drop, just like you didn't. I'm sorry for blaming you for bad aftercare. I understand why you avoided me sometimes. I wasn't good to you, either. I did hurtful things to get your attention. I'm sorry. Please understand.

As he typed the heartfelt words—and finally admitted that he carried part of the blame for their breakup—hot tears spilled down his cheeks. It was too easy to cry when you'd already cried; that was the problem.

That's nice, said Court. *But you still want to do hurtful things. Hurting me gets you off. Admit it.*

Lucan curled up more tightly under the covers and wrestled with the truth. He'd been telling himself he liked to be claimed—that was why he wanted to play those jealousy games. But seeing Court twisted up over him—not right now, but in less grave circumstances—did have its appeal.

A little, but not like this. I want to respect your limits

Okay

Just "okay"?

What do you want me to say? I feel awful right now. I'm fantasizing about how I'd feel if I'd never pestered you for your number at that stupid party.

Court was just being cruel now, telling Lucan he wanted to *erase* him. Lucan could still feel how his stomach had tumbled when he'd first caught Court's eye at that college party. They'd been so young, so ignorant. It had been a wonderful, horrible ride, but Lucan wouldn't take it back. He'd fantasized about it, sure, when they'd broken up. But those experiences with Court had helped him understand himself and had led him to fellow kinksters.

He still had more to learn about kink. This second mess was testament to that.

Please don't say you wish we'd never dated.

What if it's true?

The words enveloped Lucan in tiny, pricking spikes, draining the last bit of delusional hope he'd been holding on to. It didn't matter that he'd become enlightened in the truck with Flame. He and Court had still had a terrible fight, and Lucan could not get past it on his own. Court held all the power now, and he was saying terrible things.

Trembling, Lucan asked: *Are we breaking up?* And he waited hours for Court to answer, but no reply came.

CHAPTER 16

COURT COULDN'T MAKE himself talk to Lucan. A wall stood thick and menacing between them, and he couldn't find the mental resolve to climb over it—no matter how many times he looked at Lucan's pitiful text: *Are we breaking up?*

Were they? Should they? If they stayed together, could they make each other happy, or would it be endless cycles of these extreme highs and lows that Court wasn't sure he could weather any more of?

The days passed while Court failed to answer those questions. He worked, took on extra shifts. When his boss made him take days off, he exercised too much and watched hours of bad TV. He got a call from the testing center and listened to just enough of the voicemail to understand that his blood tests had come back negative. Cool. But it wasn't like he even wanted to think about sex lately.

Cally gave him pitying looks and had probably deduced what had happened, but Court couldn't stomach confirming it for her. She had insinuated that things with Lucan wouldn't work out, and she had been right.

Weeks after he and Lucan had last spoken—and on the night of the Deviant Desires party—Court got some texts from Cally after he finished his work shift. The first one said, *Lucan's here.* Then: *I told him you were at work, and he wanted to wait. I said that would make me uncomfortable, so he's waiting outside.* Then Cally had sent a photo showing Lucan on the stone steps of their apartment building, sitting on his knees with his hands behind his back.

It wasn't a great photo; Cally had clearly taken it through the main entrance's storm door screen. But seeing Lucan in the classically submissive pose, waiting patiently on the hard surface which couldn't be comfortable, had an emotion Court barely recognized enveloping him like a cloud: peace. This was how things were supposed to be. Court's submissive should be devoted, willing to please his Alpha despite discomfort to himself—and embarrassment, considering any of the other people who lived in the building could walk past him.

Court had started work at 3:00, and the texts had started a little after 5:00.

He replied to Cally. *When did he leave?*

Still here. I offered him food and water an hour ago, but he said no.

Heaviness throbbed through Court's body, anchoring him to the tile floor of the locker room. It was after midnight, but Lucan was still waiting for him. Was he still on his knees?

Court didn't hurry home. It wasn't that he didn't appreciate that Lucan was uncomfortable and probably looking for relief. It was that he wanted to hold on to this sweet blend of serenity and satisfaction for as long as possible because there was no telling how things would go when he and Lucan were face-to-face again. Probably, they'd combust like always. Probably, this was just a show—a way for Lucan to get back into Court's good graces so he could focus only on his own pleasure again.

Court drove a little more slowly.

At the apartment building, he parked in his assigned space and headed to the building's main entrance. Sure enough, there was Lucan, sitting in that same submissive pose, spine curved, shoulders slumped, chin against his chest.

Court ascended the steps and stopped right in front of Lucan.

Slowly, Lucan lifted his head. He looked exhausted, the porch light exaggerating the bags under his eyes.

"What is this?" Court asked.

"For—" Lucan cleared his throat, which must be incredibly dry. "For you."

Court longed to touch Lucan, to give him a comforting reward for this gesture. But he needed to know more about Lucan's motives. "Why?"

"To show you I'm serious about being your sub."

"And why do you want to be my sub?"

"Nobody else can handle me." The answers seemed to come easily, but then, Lucan had had a lot of time to think out here. He must have searched within himself for strong reasons to keep sitting and waiting.

Court crouched so he was on Lucan's level. "I can only handle you if you trust me and respect my feelings."

"I can do those things, Alpha, if..." Lucan flicked his gaze away and back again. "If you can do them in return. I need your forgiveness for breaking up with you." His eyes glistened in the sparse nighttime light. "You said you were going on instinct with me. I was, too, and sometimes our instincts were wrong, but we can do better now. Right, Alpha?"

Court couldn't stop himself from reaching out this time. He ran his thumb gently down Lucan's cheek and across his pouty bottom lip. He liked how Lucan had phrased his plea—with *we* instead of *you*. No more *you didn't give me aftercare* or *you had sex with someone else after I dumped you*. Court figured if Lucan could forgive him for those things, then Court could forgive Lucan for the breakup.

"Yes, baby. We can do better."

The relief slid off Lucan in a big, sweet wave. He dropped his hands from behind his back and set them on the stone, whining pitifully as he swayed forward into Court's crouching form.

Court stood and carefully helped Lucan to his feet. The whining only got louder and sadder as Lucan's body readjusted to movement.

Court would have liked to take Lucan up into a bridal hold to minimize his pain, but then he wouldn't have enough limbs to get Lucan inside. So he slung one of Lucan's arms over his shoulder and let him lean heavily against his side.

"I need to go to the bathroom," said Lucan. "Your sister tried to give me water, but I already had to go..."

"Shh. I'll take you right there."

They headed inside, into Court's apartment, past Cally's room, and into the bathroom. As soon as they'd crossed the bathroom's threshold, Lucan lunged toward the toilet, freed his dick, and—

Court managed to turn his back just before the stream hit the bowl.

"Fuck," Lucan said, voice full of breath. "Never been happier to piss in my life." But as soon as the stream stopped, he whined again.

Court came up behind Lucan to help him put his dick back into his jeans. This must have been erotic for him, because his noises turned soft and low, and he pushed back into Court's chest and stomach.

"Alpha," he said.

Court very slowly zipped up Lucan's fly. "Do you like being pathetic like this? Like me helping you piss and walk?"

"Yes." Lucan leaned his head back over Court's shoulder. "Missed you. Missed you in my skin."

Court smiled. "You went without me fine for six years, but a few weeks is too much, huh?"

"I wasn't fine." Lucan shook his head. "It wasn't fine."

"Shh." Court rubbed Lucan's chest in what he hoped was a calming manner. "Would you like to take a bath with me? Soothe those achy legs?"

"Yes, but..."

Court rubbed up to Lucan's throat and held it gently. "What is it?"

"Hungry. Thirsty..."

Ah. "Of course. I'll get you something, baby."

* * *

Lucan was more endorphin-drunk sitting on Court's bed eating a sandwich than he'd ever been in his life—mostly because Court was feeding it to him bite by bite. He'd cut the basic ham and cheese into little squares before bringing it to the bedroom, and the way he pressed each soft and cool bite past Lucan's lips pulled Lucan deeper into the submissive headspace he'd fallen into while waiting all that time on the hard, gray stone of Court's apartment building.

He was still stiff and achy from holding the same position for so long, but he was perfectly capable of feeding himself. Court must have realized that, and yet he still indulged Lucan's desire to feel pathetic. Lucan had known this about himself—that he wanted to feel lower than his Dom, degraded and cared for at the same time—but Court had never done this for him. And he was doing it so right.

"You're flushed." As Lucan swallowed the last bite of the sandwich, Court stroked down his throat to his collarbones, following the touch with his eyes. He regarded Lucan like a fascinating science subject doing something wonderful and unexpected. "Tell me how you're feeling right now."

"High," said Lucan. "Submissive. It's deeper than usual. I don't know, Alpha."

"Tell me more. Try harder. Ramble like you do."

I'm so grateful. Wanna pay you back for loving me, wanna get on my knees again, lick your boots, make you come. Come on me, want you to come on me. Use me. Hollow me out, fill me up, kick me. Kick me. Hold me, touch me. Let me kiss you. Let me give you whatever you want. Let me—

Lucan realized he wasn't obeying Court's orders, and fear bloomed at having to voice his desires out loud. He wanted nothing more than to please Court right now, but what if something he said made Court mad? What if Court accused him of being selfish again, of caring only about his own pleasure? Because that was where everything was coming from—his burning, aching core, but it didn't bother him that he burned and ached, that his cock was hard and had been for a while. He didn't want to be touched there if it didn't please Court, but would Court believe that?

He whimpered and crawled toward his Alpha, grabbing and nuzzling and hiding in his neck. That submissive headiness was slipping from his grasp, and he hated himself for it. Court would be displeased. Court would think the hours Lucan had waited on the porch were an act or a game.

Court rubbed Lucan's back. "Why won't you talk to me?"

"I'll say something wrong."

"No, baby. All I need is the truth."

"But I want things, I want—" He shook his head. "I'm not supposed to want, I'm just supposed to give. I'll say the wrong thing. You'll be mad again."

"Lucan." Court gripped Lucan's shoulders and gave him a shake. "You're thinking too hard. I give orders, and you obey them. That's all you need to do. That's all you need to worry about."

For not the first time, Lucan recalled Court saying similar words in the past. *"I give the orders, you obey them. I ask questions, you answer them."* Lucan realized now that he'd never fully submitted to Court. He'd always fought him on something, always pushed. But just a few minutes ago, he'd tasted what it could be like if he gave in utterly. Court encircling him, holding him up, saying sweet, mean things to him. Court feeding him, nurturing him, making him heady with invasive, loving attention.

Lucan didn't have anything left to worry about, did he? "Did the testing center call you?"

"Mhm. Clean."

"Me, too. And we're for sure staying together?"

"Yes, Lucan."

"And you still love me?"

Court smiled in a long-suffering way. "Yes, I love you."

Lucan took a deep breath and exhaled slowly. "Okay. You give the orders. I obey them. I understand, Alpha."

Court narrowed his eyes, searching Lucan's gaze. He must have found what he wanted there, because eventually, he nodded. "Good." He pushed Lucan's hair back, stroking his scalp with the perfect amount of pressure until the skin tingled. "Now, tell me one of the things you want that you don't think you're supposed to want."

Nerves clawed at Lucan's stomach, but he pushed past the feeling. "I want you to come on me."

Court's nostrils flared.

What kind of game was this? Was Court going to give Lucan what he wanted now? Was he going to shove him to the floor, whip out that thick, perfect—

Court gripped Lucan's hair and teased him with his lips. He almost kissed him but not quite, then brushed their lips together just barely, then finally kissed him, but it was soft, gentle, the lightest of touches that could still be called a kiss. "Good boy."

Lucan's body tensed with need, his sensations boiling down to the burn in his scalp from Court's grip and the throbbing, swollen tightness of his lower stomach and groin. But his mind went quiet. Uninhibited, he let his gaze rove over Court's face, taking in every freckle, dip, and curve. He touched him, stroking the bridge of his nose, tracing his lips.

Court smiled and let go of Lucan's hair to massage his scalp instead. It felt so good that Lucan found himself closing his eyes and drifting...

"'Come on me,' he says, then goes to sleep," Court teased.

Lucan came back to life and shoved at Court playfully.

Court took Lucan's wrists. "Bath time."

"Whatever you say, Alpha."

Court's eyes glinted. "You're finally getting it, aren't you, baby?" He held Lucan's hand all the way to the bathroom and didn't let go until he had to take off his clothes.

In the bathtub, sitting on top of Court in the warm water, Lucan found it even harder to stay awake. Then Court started washing his hair, his strong hands massaging Lucan's scalp again.

"It's okay if you doze," said Court. "I got you."

For the first time—ever—Lucan actually believed those words; Court *did* have him safely in hand.

CHAPTER 17

FOR THE NEXT MONTH, Court saw Lucan whenever he could. The best part about it was that Lucan seemed equally interested in seeing Court, and he didn't complain when Court had them doing "vanilla" things like going to the movies and dinner and binge-watching TV shows before getting early-morning donuts for old time's sake. They did kinky things, too, but it was all in good fun—no punishments.

At the TNG party, Court had Lucan wear a butt plug, and though they didn't do any public scening, it was gratifying to watch him squirm while socializing with a pretty flush to his cheeks that never left. Afterward, Court took Lucan home and fucked him slowly for hours, staving off his orgasm with a cock ring that encircled his dick and balls. They found heady oblivion together, Court's awareness centering only on Lucan and his chants of "Yes, Alpha," "No, Alpha," "Please," and "Come in me." Lucan had been so tired afterward that he'd fallen asleep before Court, and Court finally understood why Lucan sniped at him for always passing out right after sex. It was lonely being the only one awake, but it was only for a few minutes, and Court got to watch Lucan in his moment of absolute peace, sacked out after experiencing a wonderful high at Court's hand.

When they talked about the scene the next morning, Lucan couldn't seem to shut up about how great it had felt to have Court come in him and feel the spend leaking out of him afterward. Court apologized for not taking care of the STI testing earlier, and Lucan kissed his face all over and poured out sweet words of forgiveness.

When they met up at the Deviant Desires party a week later, though, Lucan was in a mood. He trailed into the bar after Dom, Roland, and Erin with his arms crossed and his face set in a scowl. Court had been one of the first to arrive and had been sitting at one of the tables by himself for about a half hour nursing a Diet Coke. To his surprise, Lucan and his roommates took up the rest of the table's seats, with Roland pulling up an extra chair for Erin.

Roland, whom Court had only seen in passing, smiled genially and held out a hand. "Hey, Court. Great to finally meet you. I'm Roland."

Court shook his hand. "Great to meet you, too." He probably sounded less than enthusiastic, but Roland, Dom, and Erin were all staring at him, and it kind of made him want to hightail it far away from this table.

Lucan was pouting with his jaw in his hand and staring off into the distance.

"This is Erin," said Roland and gestured to her. "She's in littlespace and doesn't like talking to people she doesn't know that well. It's not personal, though."

"Oh. Sure," said Court. "Totally understandable."

Erin was still watching Court, though, and she really did give off the energy of a little kid despite the generous cleavage of her V-neck. Roland reached into a leather bag on the floor and pulled out a children's book with a dog on the cover.

Erin grinned and snatched the book.

Court remembered his own sub and leaned to whisper into Lucan's ear, but as soon as Lucan noticed him getting closer, he scooted his chair back.

Fine; Court wouldn't whisper. "What's gotten into you?"

"Nothing," Lucan sniped.

"He's mad because I'm moving out," said Dom. "Even though he's *not* the reason." Dom was clearly directing his words at Lucan. "I've been planning to leave the lifestyle for years."

Court wanted to ask why Dom was at this party if he was leaving the lifestyle but refrained. He also wanted to know why Lucan was throwing such a fit if what he and Dom had had together was *platonic*.

Wordlessly, Lucan got up from the table and headed toward the bar.

Court gave Lucan's friends as charming a smile as he could muster before following him. He slid onto the barstool next to him. "Does this have anything to do with the fact that I haven't beaten you lately?" Court had been expecting a little moodiness from Lucan because of that. He had been meaning to give him a punishment, but he'd been so happy that inspiration had been hard to come by.

"Well, that's definitely not helping, *Alpha*." Lucan said the honorific with such disrespect that suddenly Court had all the inspiration in the world.

But he wasn't going to punish Lucan for being upset. "Tell me about Dom moving out."

"He's so full of shit." Lucan glanced in the direction of the table where Roland, Dom, and Erin were still sitting. "He says it's not my fault that he's moving out and won't be coming to parties after tonight, but come on. I stopped being his play partner, and now he's doing all this? There's no way it's not connected."

"Yeah, it's probably connected. But who cares?"

Lucan's brow scrunched into a deep vee. "I do."

"I know, baby, I just mean... It's his decision. And if it's because of you, oh well. What are you going to do? Leave me and go back to him?"

"Obviously not."

"Then you'll just have to deal with it. It is what it is. And he probably does have other reasons besides what happened with you for leaving." Court picked at the skin around his nails. "I, for one, am glad to see him go." When he looked up from his nails, it was to find Lucan staring at him. "What?"

"Are you jealous?"

Court sighed. He hadn't told Lucan about Dom confronting him weeks before, and he didn't want to. But he also didn't want to come off like an ass. He could be jealous, but not about this. "Dom kind of bombarded me in your kitchen after I belted you that one night. Said you teaching me about BDSM wasn't going to work and there were other people in the lifestyle better for you."

Lucan threw his head back. "*Why* am I not surprised?" But he seemed less upset, at least. After a few beats, he asked, "What did you say back to him?" Lucan's gaze held a flirty, fascinated gleam now, and Court got the feeling he was supposed to say something sexy.

Well, he only had the truth. "I told him if he thought somebody needed to keep an eye on me that he could watch me fuck you."

Lucan's eyes crinkled happily. "You didn't."

"That's actually almost a quote."

"I love you." It was only the second time Lucan had said the words, and the casual nature of them—how they just seemed to spill out—warmed Court's chest.

"I love you, too," he said.

Lucan slid a hand onto Court's thigh. "Are you in the mood to play with me tonight? Here?"

Court had been wanting to try playing publicly for a while now, but having the possibility posed to him had nerves swelling in his stomach. "Sure."

"You look scared."

"I'm not *scared*."

"It's okay if you are. It can be intimidating, but once you start scening, you kind of forget about everybody around."

Court didn't usually care what other people thought. But in coming up with what to do to Lucan, which he never had trouble with when they were alone, what if he didn't do the "right" things the "right" way? The last thing he needed was Dom or another one of Lucan's friends confronting him again when he was busy trying to take care of Lucan and soak in the good feelings that came after a scene.

Though it felt like Lucan had sort of stepped back from being Court's teacher, Court deferred to him in this. "What kind of play is appropriate here?"

"A lot of people do impact. Spanking, flogging, etc. And they don't usually have sex, but that's not technically against the rules."

Lucan had insinuated that he needed punished soon, but Court couldn't imagine belting Lucan in front of everyone. Punishments were for dark, private places—for them only. A few weeks ago, Court had stashed his leather gloves in his car in case he got inspired to give Lucan a spanking. He wanted to be able to wail on Lucan without his palm burning afterward, and this might be a good time to do that.

"Okay. I just need to get something from my car first," he said.

Lucan fished an object out of his tight jeans pocket—a metal something made out of four little silver balls. "We can use these if you'd like."

"Huh?"

Lucan smiled and pulled one of the balls away from the other three. "They're nipple clamps. Magnets. They're strong, and they hurt good."

"Yeah, okay." Court glanced toward the dark doorway of the playroom and tried not to feel like Lucan's lesson plans were culminating in a test. He slid off his barstool. "I'll be right back."

"Okay, Alpha." But Lucan pulled Court back with a tug on his hand to kiss him on the cheek. "It'll be fine. We'll have fun."

"Fun," Court echoed.

* * *

Lucan was excited to play with Court, but he had an ulterior motive for asking him to play publicly: he wanted everyone—including Dom—to see how perfect his Dominant was. When Court came back inside wearing black leather gloves along with his military-style, short-sleeved button-up that perfectly showed off his biceps, Lucan felt like a swooning woman in a black-and-white movie. Court was so fucking hot.

Court approached the bar. "You're looking at me like you wanna eat me."

Lucan swallowed and slid off his stool. "I do."

Court gave a cocky smile. "Let's go see if there are any spanking benches available."

The last time someone had spanked Lucan in public had been over a year ago, and it had been Flame. Back then, Lucan's nerves beforehand had been sickly and scared, but now, he was buzzing with excitement, his mind racing with expectations. There would be no underwear staying on, Lucan was pretty sure. Court would bare his ass and beat him until he was screaming, crying, or coming—or all three. At least, Lucan hoped. Would Court go easy on him because of the spectators?

Lucan followed Court into the playroom. The vibing beat of the music did its part to narrow Lucan's focus onto the here and now. On one side of the large room, a spanking bench stood empty, and Court headed straight for it.

With those strong, gloved hands, he grabbed Lucan and manhandled him onto the bench. The unexpected forcefulness had Lucan falling hard into the scene, his heartbeat throbbing with the music.

"Alpha, the clamps." Lucan produced the little magnets and held them out to Court.

Court yanked Lucan back so that he was on his knees on the bench's supports. "Put them on yourself," he said and held Lucan up so he wouldn't lose his balance.

On the spot, Lucan fumbled with the balls and his shirt. But he'd been smart in choosing a loose tank tonight, and Court let him use a gloved palm to rest half the magnets while he put the first two in place. It had been a while now since Lucan had worn clamps, and the magnets' pinching was harsh and pointed enough to make him hiss.

"They'll stay on when you squirm?" Court asked.

"Should be fine."

"Undo your jeans."

Lucan obeyed.

Then Court lowered him back down onto the spanking bench and immediately yanked off his pants and underwear, leaving them bunched around his thighs.

A certain sense of safety washed over Lucan. This was familiar now —Court's impatient dominance—and Lucan knew he was going to get the pain he wanted and that he wouldn't have to wait very long for it. He didn't have to wonder or anticipate like he'd always done with Dom, and he didn't have to grow bored and disconnected like he had with Flame. It was nothing against them—there were subs who'd love to be on the receiving end of their play—but Lucan was damn grateful to have a Dominant on his wavelength. He was grateful to have Court.

The hits started hard and stayed hard. Court's gloves dulled the sting a little, but they did nothing to diminish the thudding impact that would no doubt leave Lucan with bruises. The onslaught complemented the pinching pain in Lucan's nipples, and he fell away, swimming in the sensations and his worry-free trust in Court.

The hits stopped. A moment later, Court resumed them with his bare hand, bringing an irresistible, stinging heat to Lucan's skin.

After a while—Lucan didn't know how long—Court paused and pressed his clothed groin to Lucan's ass. His fly was rough against Lucan's lit-up skin. He folded over his back, panting near his ear. "Okay, baby?"

"Green."

"You're being such a good bottom for me. Making pretty noises for all your friends to hear."

Lucan had forgotten about where they were and who might be watching. Now, he looked up and saw the shapes of people, but he clamped his eyes shut before he could see their faces.

Court got off him, then yanked him to his knees again, exposing Lucan's hard cock. He inspected his nipples, probably making sure they still looked pink and healthy. The magnets had stayed perfectly in place.

He shoved Lucan back down and resumed the spanking with his bare hand. The pain sharpened to a degree that made Lucan tremble and whimper. Court scratched harshly across the angry skin until Lucan was moaning and rutting against the spanking bench.

Court walked around the bench until he was standing in front of Lucan's face. Lucan had his cheek rested against the bench's vinyl, and though he wasn't crying, he was on the cusp of it. At the same time, endorphins soaked his brain, and he smiled.

Court tapped Lucan's nose with his ungloved hand. "Tell me if this sounds good to you. Are you listening, baby?"

"Yes, Alpha."

Court stroked Lucan's cheek and traced his lips. Though his touches remained sweet and affectionate, his gaze glittered darkly. "What if we go to your place, and I treat you like the whore you are?"

Lucan sunk deeper into Court's clutches. He'd been wanting this—the darkness they'd left behind with their last fight—but he hadn't wanted to tarnish things or turn Court off.

"Yes, please," he whispered.

Court smiled and walked around the bench again. He helped Lucan off it, pulled up his pants for him, and carefully removed the nipple clamps. Pain bloomed in the abused peaks as blood rushed back into them. Lucan's eyes welled, and he leaned back into Court's strong frame.

As Court rubbed him down, Lucan registered fully the people watching them. Nearby, Dom leaned against a wooden support with his arms crossed, expression softer than it had been in weeks—and pained. Maybe he was realizing how mismatched he and Lucan had been as play partners. Court had hardly done his worst, but pain had still been his focus. What would Dom think if he knew what Lucan and Court got up to in private? But of course, he'd been in the house when Lucan had gotten his last punishment. Lucan's anxiety flared as he remembered what Flame had relayed from Dom—that all his roommates had heard Lucan scream.

He didn't usually worry about what noises he made during public scenes—some people were truly obnoxious about it, and he figured he wasn't—but had he been with Court?

"You're okay." Court must have sensed his distress.

Part of Lucan regretted suggesting they play in public. "Wanna be alone with you, Alpha."

"That's where we're going."

As they made their way toward the mouth of the playroom, Lucan spotted Roland and Erin on a couch. Roland caught his eye and gave him a smile and a wink. Even Erin gave Lucan a grin around the big sucker in her mouth. The subtle shows of support warmed Lucan.

Court tugged Lucan by the hand out of the bar and to the parking lot. Maybe it was the fact that he was already emotional from playing, but his chest pinched as he remembered following Court out here just a few months ago. That first time they'd had sex after their years apart had been so different from how things felt between them now, and yet it hadn't been that long ago. It scared Lucan how easily relationships could come together and fall apart.

When they got to the car and Court let go of his hand, Lucan pulled him back. "Babe." It was what he'd used to call Court in college.

"What is it?" Court asked.

"I'm— I'm really struggling with, like—"

Court waited patiently while Lucan tried to get it out.

"I really love you. I'm—I'm not confused anymore about what that feels like because the idea of losing you makes me want to fucking die." He realized as the words fell out that they were wildly and painfully true. "You have to collar me, Court. You have to actually keep me forever this time. We can't have some ridiculous fight and then you begging me back or me sitting on my knees on your porch for hours doesn't work. We have to go collar shopping as soon as possible, or we can order one online tonight. You have to—"

"Okay. It's okay." Court pulled Lucan into a hug. "We're not going to break up again."

Lucan drank in the physical contact, and his eyes fluttered closed. "It's just like, everything is so fucking fragile."

"I know, but we're not anymore. You don't have to be scared." Court rubbed Lucan's back in gentle circles. "When your ass is flabby and wrinkled, I'll still be spanking it."

Lucan laughed into Court's shoulder. "Shut up."

"It's true."

The panic that had tried to drown Lucan slipped away. He breathed in the subtle, masculine scent of Court's cologne and realized they were wasting time in this parking lot when they should be taking advantage of an empty house.

He pulled back and kissed Court. "Let's go play."

Court searched his eyes. "You still up for it? We can cuddle instead."

"I'm up for it."

In the car a few minutes later, Lucan realized what would make their play tonight even better. His ass cheeks were sore, yeah, but Court had barely scratched the surface of his mind. "When we get home, would you be all right with me resisting you? You said we could try the bratty thing."

Court took a few beats to answer. "Yeah, I think so."

"If you don't like how things are going, call yellow, and we'll change course. Or red. Safewords are for you, too."

Court gave Lucan one of his charming smiles. "Thanks, baby. I'll keep that in mind."

CHAPTER 18

OUTSIDE LUCAN'S HOUSE, Court jogged around to the other side of the car and opened Lucan's door for him. The perturbed look he leveled at him was exactly what Court had been going for.

"Putting on the charm before you fuck me up, huh?" Lucan asked.

Court didn't answer. He simply stood back from the car, hand on the open door, and waited for Lucan to exit. His plan, made up on the fly while he'd been driving, was to pull them into a roleplay-type of situation without explicitly telling Lucan that. He wanted him on edge, and he wanted to get to that place they'd been when he'd told Lucan he'd fantasized about keeping him prisoner.

Maybe he was being bad going on instinct like he'd used to do. But he knew Lucan's limits now, and they had safewords. Like Lucan had said, if either one of them didn't like how things were going, they could call red or yellow and come back to reality.

But Court hoped they could go so deep into it that reality wouldn't matter.

He walked Lucan to the door. "I had a good time tonight. On our date," Court said with emphasis, trying to give Lucan a hint as to his intentions.

Over his shoulder, Lucan gave Court an unsettled look but then turned his back on the door instead of going right in. "Um. Me, too."

"You don't sound sincere. Didn't I show you a good time, Lucan?" Court stepped into Lucan's personal space, and it had the desired effect; Lucan stiffened.

"Yeah, of course," he said.

It still sounded like a lie, and Court couldn't help but grin. He was going for a predator feel, though, so the self-satisfied grin wasn't completely out of character.

He brushed Lucan's chin and closed the distance between them for a light kiss. It was exactly how he'd kiss someone at the end of a good first date.

Lucan, bless him, melted. But at the end of the kiss, he recovered and stepped backward until he bumped into the storm door.

"Invite me inside," said Court.

"No." Lucan turned in the small space he had available to him and fumbled for his keys.

Court deftly took them from him and snaked an arm around Lucan's waist from behind.

Lucan made a sad, scared sound.

"Shh," said Court. Where his nose connected with the back of Lucan's ear, the flesh was burning hot.

Yes. This was exactly the kind of reaction Court had been looking for.

"Court." Lucan's tone was naked and real despite the fact that he hadn't called yellow. "Tell me what you're going to do to me."

Court took advantage of Lucan's hesitation to unlock and open the door. "I don't know yet, and even if I did, I wouldn't tell you."

"Can I make a request, though?"

Court hadn't planned on taking anymore *requests* tonight, but he found that he wasn't annoyed. Whatever Lucan suggested would probably make this better.

In the foyer, he crossed his arms. "Go ahead."

"I've been wanting..." He scratched the back of his neck. "I've been wondering what it would be like if you put me on the floor and kicked me."

It took a second for the words to compute. Court definitely hadn't seen anything like that in porn, and he'd never heard of it mentioned in a kink space. Would Lucan really like that?

"You hate the idea," said Lucan.

Court shut and locked the door, blocking out the porch light and bathing them in darkness.

Lucan flipped on a switch.

Court didn't *hate* Lucan's request. He just wasn't sure he understood it, but what was the harm in trying it? They had tried all sorts of things lately, and they'd come out whole every time.

He put his predator face back on and yanked Lucan toward him. "Did you really think you could tease me all night and not invite me in?"

Lucan struggled in Court's hold. "I don't owe you a fuck!"

Court laughed at Lucan's inventiveness. And he was finding he quite liked the resistance. It was...cute, in its way. Because the truth was Lucan could never resist Court, even when he tried.

"You owe me a lot more than a fuck." Court had never pushed someone to the floor before—aside from a nudge or two to show them he wanted his dick sucked. But, despite feeling awkward, he pushed Lucan down, and when Lucan resisted, he shoved harder. Not too hard —he didn't want to throw him down there—but Lucan still fell to the floorboards.

Lucan looked up at him expectantly.

Court exhaled, relieved. He nudged Lucan with his shoe as a test. When Lucan just stared at Court's foot, obviously unimpressed, he kicked him harder, then a little harder than that. He didn't want to hurt him—not in any serious way—but he increased the violence of the act until Lucan went boneless on the floor and moaned.

Lucan's pleasure gave Court a rush. He crouched and gripped Lucan's chin. "You like it when I treat you like dirt under my shoe?"

"Yes, Alpha." He reached out to Court. "Can we not pretend we're other people? Will you be mean as you?"

Court felt like he was on a train Lucan was driving, which was bullshit. He needed to wrestle back control. But wasn't Lucan adorable making messed-up requests in that sweet, submissive voice?

"Are you sure you want me to be mean for real?" Court asked. "We've been having fun."

"But we've worked out all our issues, right? Do what you said you were going to do. Treat me like the whore I am. I *need* it." Lucan's voice got rough over the word *need*, and he leaned his head back, limbs loose on the hardwood.

Court wasn't sure they'd gotten past every fucked-up thing between them. It was possible that through this play they'd find another stumbling block, trip, and hurt themselves. But Lucan was asking for something, and Court just didn't have it in him anymore to refuse Lucan his desires.

He stood tall and bore his gaze into Lucan's prone form. "What kind of whore do you want to be?" Using the wall for support, he rested his shoe on Lucan's chest. "Should I treat you like a commodity I'm lucky to afford?" He stepped just a little harder. "Or do you want to feel like a bit of trash I picked up in alley for a twenty-dollar skullfuck?"

Lucan breathed faster, his chest rising and falling against Court's foot. "You know the answer."

"That's right. Look at you." Court gave a disgusted scoff. "You asked me to put you on the floor and kick you. You know who does that? Abusive boyfriends." He gave Lucan another calculated kick to the ribs. "You want to be my battered little housewife, baby? You want me to spank you if the floor isn't as clean as I like?"

Lucan whimpered and gripped Court's calf, his warm fingers teasing under the hem of his trousers. The affectionate gesture twisted through Court, stiffening his chest.

He bent down, yanked Lucan up, and shoved him against the wall.

Lucan pawed at Court's face—gentle, sweet—and Court pressed his knee between his legs, earning him a breathy moan.

"You wanted to be a brat and fight me tonight, but you can't, can you?" Court asked.

"You're right. I can't, I can't." Lucan nuzzled Court's face, kissed his cheek, his lips.

An intense rush of affection hit Court, and the beast inside him reared its head and screamed, *Feed me!* He gave Lucan savage kisses, biting at his pretty mouth, jaw, neck. He hiked up Lucan's legs and gave him a fresh shove to the wall, and Lucan's soft little touches turned to scratches, pain at the back of Court's neck.

"So hot for me tonight, aren't you, baby?" Court asked.

Lucan nodded. "I'm just so proud of you."

It was the last thing Court expected to hear right now, and it stopped him in his tracks. He looked into Lucan's serene gaze. "Yeah?"

"Yeah, you're so great. I can ask you for the most messed-up things, and it's still safe." Lucan petted Court's face, lips, neck. "You take such good care of me. You were so good to me at the party, and you're so good to me now. I love you. I love you so much."

Fuck. Was this supposed to be a turn-on? Because Court's cock was harder than ever listening to that little monologue.

He rutted hard again Lucan's clothed groin.

"Want you so bad," Lucan half whispered in a broken voice, and Court was quickly moving beyond calculated decisions. He just wanted to be inside Lucan, wanted to own him, have him, keep him.

He pulled him away from the wall, and Lucan wrapped his arms and legs tightly around Court's waist. As Court carried him up the stairs, he grunted with the exertion, and Lucan rambled in sweet whispers about how strong and attractive Court was and how much he wanted to be under him, filled by him, held, ruined.

By the time he was throwing Lucan onto the bed and tearing both their clothes off, he was so aroused he could barely think.

Lucan shoved lube into Court's hand, but Court pushed back. "Prepare yourself for me."

"Yes, Alpha."

That title falling from Lucan's lips calmed Court. Though he still throbbed with need, his focus narrowed to Lucan's exposed hole and wet fingers lubing and stretching himself. The slick sounds were beautifully obscene.

Once Lucan was moaning and enthusiastically fucking himself, Court grabbed him, tearing him from his task, and forced him onto his stomach. He lined up his cock and shoved himself in.

Lucan yelled and dug into the blankets.

"Thank me," Court growled. He fucked Lucan hard and deep, and Lucan whined and writhed under him.

"Thank you," Lucan moaned. "Thank you, thank you."

Court wrapped his arm around Lucan's chest and held him tight while he continued to spear him. Somehow, this felt more intimate than their face-to-face fucks, and he got lost in the naked heat and friction.

After a while, he slowed down his thrusts. Lucan tried to reach under himself, but Court stopped him, taking his hands and pinning them against the mattress.

"I'll get you there," he said.

"Please, more." Court knew by now that when Lucan said *more*, he almost always meant *hurt me*.

Court went for the easiest thing in the moment—and something he hadn't fully explored with Lucan yet. He took a firm handful of his dyed-blond hair with its dark roots and gripped, tugging his head back.

Lucan's lips parted, and his eyes fell closed. "Alpha..."

"You like that?"

Lucan only hummed.

Court kept the hold and resumed fucking Lucan's perfect ass. Every once in a while, he'd shove Lucan's head down and give his scalp a rest, but then he'd take a firm grip again. The last time he let go, he ran his finger softly over Lucan's scalp.

Lucan's whole body shivered, and he made a high-pitched sound. "Oh, God, that's intense. I'm gonna come, Alpha."

Court pressed flush to Lucan's back and panted against his ear. "Good." He snapped his hips a few times as hard as he could, and Lucan screamed, his body shuddering violently. Even after he went limp, his muscles gave a few little jumps and twitches.

Court pulled out and rolled Lucan onto his back. His cock was painfully hard now. He found the bottle of lube in the blankets and slicked himself up.

Lucan just watched him—silent, peaceful.

Court stroked himself as quickly as he could. When he moaned, Lucan moaned, too—erotic and adorable at the same time.

"Gonna come on you," Court warned.

"I know." Despite the fact that Lucan's cock lay soft and spent, he was breathing hard again and squirming. "I want it, I want it."

The display pushed Court over the edge. Pleasure gripped him, tensing and jerking all his muscles, and the most primal parts of him reveled in his cum spurting onto Lucan's neck, chin, and lips.

Lucan moaned like he was having another orgasm. It was the most endearing thing Court had ever seen.

When his own pleasure subsided, exhaustion hit him, and he collapsed onto his side next to Lucan.

Lucan continued to breathe hard for several minutes, and Court's eyelids grew heavy.

"No, no, no." Lucan tapped Court's cheek. "Don't leave me yet. Please, Alpha."

Court groaned and sat up. If he wasn't going to fall asleep, he couldn't be lying next to his favorite person after claiming him so thoroughly. He reached for the box of tissues on the nightstand and cleaned his cum from Lucan's face and neck.

"You didn't have to wipe it off yet," said Lucan.

"When did you become obsessed with cum?"

"Just yours."

Court smiled and shook his head.

"Am I getting annoying?" Lucan stroked gentle fingertips over Court's forearm. "With all my feelings and how into you I am?"

Court stared down at Lucan, marveling at how this beautiful man could think his affection would ever annoy Court. "Are you kidding? I love it."

"Okay." But Lucan averted a pained gaze; he clearly didn't believe him.

"Lucan."

"What?"

"You tell me I'm so great and how I take such good care of you, but you don't believe me about this?"

Lucan sat up and snuggled against Court, hiding his face against his arm. "I don't know."

Court rubbed Lucan's back and kissed the top of his head. "Your affection made what we just did very good for me." He petted Lucan's head, squeezed the back of his neck. "You felt my orgasm in your own body, didn't you?"

Lucan nodded.

Court realized Lucan had been right about safe, sane, and consensual kink. This—talking about the scene afterward—was becoming second nature for him. It didn't feel like a chore at all.

"Was there anything you didn't like?" Court asked.

Lucan shook his head. "All good, Alpha." He petted Court's abs. "What about you?"

"Well, I'm not really into kicking you, but if you like it, I'll do it."

"No, it's fine. It turned me on that you did it so carefully, though. And..." Lucan breathed through his mouth. "The stuff you say... I love it."

Court put a finger under Lucan's chin and guided his gaze up. "I love the stuff you say, too. When you poured out all those feelings to me, that"—Court felt his face grow hot—"praise, I had to have you. I had to show you that you're mine."

Lucan's gaze was intense on Court—almost aggressive. After a few moments, he climbed Court, pushing him onto his back. "You're so cute. I can't stand it."

Cute? Court burst out laughing. "Am I?"

"Yes!" Lucan gave Court a deep kiss. At first, it was as intense as Lucan's aggressive stare, but it tapered off, turning slow, gentle. Eventually, Lucan ended up lying with his head on Court's chest.

"Are you ready to sleep now?" Court asked.

Lucan didn't say anything for a while, and with his breathing slow and even, Court thought he might have fallen asleep already. But then he said in a heavy voice, "Thank you for coming back to me."

The words wrapped Court up like a hug, though at the same time, emotion clogged his chest. "Ditto, baby." Maybe he hadn't said enough, but if he tried to further translate the intense love he had for Lucan and how grateful he was to have him here in his arms right now, he'd probably cry.

"I am ready to sleep now," Lucan said. "Are you?"

"Mmm," Court managed. The last thing he registered was Lucan's fingertip drawing featherlight shapes over his collarbone.

* * *

Lucan tapped Court's arm. "They're turning the sign!" The sign in question hung in the front window of The Fetish Palace, and now it read "OPEN" in frilly black script. Lucan had slept so deeply after all he'd done with Court last night that he'd been wide-awake and full of energy at 8:00 a.m. this morning. He'd dragged Court out of bed for a shower, breakfast, and this.

Now, finally, the store was open, and they were going to get their collars—or collar-like jewelry, anyway.

"Good morning," said the saleswoman as they entered. Court gave her a polite response, but Lucan was too busy rushing for the collars section.

Most of the collars were leather. Lucan gravitated toward the narrower ones with subtle silver rings or charms, but he didn't want to walk around in something that looked like a choker. Court stood at Lucan's back, inspecting the collars as well, while the saleswoman hovered nearby.

"Is there something in particular you're looking for?" she asked.

"Do you have any jewelry?" Lucan fingered a heart-shaped charm that read "OWNED." "I don't know if a regular necklace would work, though. I want something fetish people would get but vanillas wouldn't be weirded out by." Lucan gave Court his cutest submissive look. "I want to wear it always. And he needs something, too," he told the saleswoman.

She squinted in thought, but then her lips spread into a confident smile. "I have something that might work." She led them over to a jewelry case. Lucan watched her hand under the glass as she plucked out a set of silver wrist cuffs.

At first, Lucan thought they were plain, but when she took them out of their little foam case, the big letters engraved in them became evident. One cuff had a *D*, and the other had an *s*.

They were perfect.

"A little big," said Court.

"But people have to be able to read the letters, babe," said Lucan.

"Would you like to try them on?" the saleswoman asked.

Lucan nodded and held out his wrist along with Court. The cuffs were adjustable, and the saleswoman bent them carefully around each of their wrists for a perfect fit.

Lucan's stomach roiled when he asked, "How much are they?"

"Don't worry about it," muttered Court.

"Forty-eight for the set. They're stainless steel," said the saleswoman.

Lucan figured if they both paid half—

"We'll take them," said Court. Immediately, he reached for his wallet. Lucan did the same, but Court stopped him with a stern palm. "Put that away. I've got it."

Guilt pricked Lucan's stomach. "Are you sure?"

"Yes. I make more money than you. Don't worry about it."

Well, that was true. Lucan took a deep breath and let the transaction happen. If Court wanted to pay, that was his business, but Lucan would repay him in obedience later.

After they'd exited the store and were on the way back to the car, Lucan hooked his arm around Court's. "Thank you for footing the bill."

"Your eyes lit up when you saw them. There was just no question."

Lucan smiled and kissed Court's cheek. Then he examined the cuff on Court's wrist, tracing its edges and the engraved *D* in its pretty script font.

"Does it look good on me?" Court asked.

"Yeah, but everything looks good on you."

They were in the parking lot now, and Court stepped back from Lucan and looked him up and down, gaze stopping on the cuff multiple times. "I think people at parties will get it."

Lucan laughed. "I'm sure if they don't, you'll tell them."

Court's eyes twinkled in the late-morning sun. "Damn right I will."

God, Lucan loved this man. It was a wild, frantic kind of feeling speeding through his chest at all hours now—both when he was with Court and when he wasn't. Probably, it would calm down with time, though Lucan didn't know anything about long-term love. Roland and Erin had been together for a few years; he'd have to ask if they still felt nuts staring at each other.

Court got into the car, and Lucan followed.

Hands on the wheel, Court asked, "Where to?"

Lucan leaned his head back and smiled at his Dominant. "Anywhere."

CHAPTER 19

ONE YEAR later

Lucan, sweaty and exhausted from carrying about a million boxes and a few large pieces of furniture from the moving truck to his and Court's new apartment, dropped onto his back on the carpeted floor and exhaled. "We survived!"

Above him, a gloriously shirtless Court came into view. "We still have to unpack."

"I know that."

"Plus, I forgot something."

"Huh?"

Court nudged Lucan with his shoe. "Come help me find it."

Lucan groaned and remained on the floor for another couple of minutes before grudgingly getting to his feet and following Court back out into the oppressive heat. They'd tried to get everything inside early to avoid the hottest part of the morning, but even now that Lucan worked at home as a blogger and freelance writer and therefore set his own hours, he had trouble getting out of bed before 10:00 a.m.

He hopped into the back of the moving truck with Court. The metal and wood interior, previously filled to the brim with boxes and other items, was a big open space now. "There's nothing in here."

"It's a little box. Help me look."

Lucan rolled his eyes but did as told, scouring the truck's nooks, crannies, and high shelves. He was about to accuse Court of being addled from too much sun and heat when he spotted something in a corner: a little velvet box like the kind that held jewelry.

His stomach clenched. This couldn't be a—an *engagement* ring, could it? Well, of course not. Court hadn't said anything about a gift for Lucan of any kind, let alone *that*. Court probably kept, like, cufflinks in there.

Lucan picked up the box and showed it to Court. "Is this what you're looking for?"

Court grinned. "Yep. Open it."

Oh, God. "Why do you want me to open this? *You* were looking for it. Here." He tried to hand the box to Court, but Court nudged his hand away.

"Open it, baby. You don't have to be scared."

Fuck. Lucan was way too dehydrated for the amount of tears that suddenly welled in his eyes and spilled down his face. But he opened the box.

It *was* an engagement ring: a simple silver band that would match his stainless steel *s* bracelet perfectly. "Court, I—"

In the dirty, hot interior of the moving truck, Court got down on one knee. "Lucan Burke, my precious submissive and the love of my life, will you please marry me?"

Lucan let out a fresh sob. Was this really happening? To *him*? He'd seen proposals before; Erin especially liked to share videos of them to her Facebook timeline, but those things were for other people. A lot of the time, Lucan still marveled at the fact that he and Court had been together over a year.

"Hey." Court was looking up at Lucan with eyes full of fear. "If this isn't what you want..."

Shit, Lucan had left him hanging! "No, it is. It is." Because if Court wanted to marry Lucan, of course Lucan would agree—even if he couldn't quite wrap his head around the idea. It wasn't like he didn't already plan on being with Court for as long as humanly possible.

He laughed through his tears and held the ring to his chest. "Yes, I'll marry you, babe."

Court's very soul seemed to light up as his lips spread into a toothy smile. He got to his feet and cupped Lucan's face with both hands. "Yeah?"

Lucan nodded vigorously. "Yes, Alpha."

Court pressed several hard pecks to Lucan's face and lips, which only made Lucan laugh harder. He must taste salty with how much he'd been crying.

"You scared the shit out of me," said Court.

"Sorry. You could have given me a hint or something."

"And ruin the surprise? No way."

Lucan shook his head. And as much as he wanted to continue to cherish this moment, he wanted to do it inside. "I need AC, babe."

They hopped out of the truck and reentered their new apartment. Lucan's mind was still struggling to accept the fact that they'd moved in together, but now... Now they were going to be husbands. *Husbands.*

The idea was big and foreign, but it was right.

Court fetched them cold bottles of water from a cooler he'd brought. When Lucan struggled to hold the ring and open his bottle at the same time, Court took the little box from him and plucked out the ring from its blue satin.

"Hold out your hand," he said.

Lucan did, and Court slipped on the ring. This was so much different than when he'd first put on his *s* bracelet. The little strip of silver was so light, yet it carried so much. Would they have a wedding? When Lucan imagined standing in front of everybody each of them loved and having Court show them all that he wanted to be with Lucan for the rest of his life, Lucan actually wobbled on his feet.

He leaned against their new stove. "Babe? Where's *your* ring?"

Court was transferring the contents of the cooler to the refrigerator, but he stopped to reach into the pocket of his basketball shorts and produced a second jewelry box.

Lucan rushed forward and snatched it from him. The ring inside was exactly like Lucan's but a little bigger to fit Court's hand. "Let me put it on you."

Court smiled and held out his hand. As Lucan slid the ring into place, he felt as if his chest would crack open with how full it was. Over the past year, he'd settled into his relationship with Court. The love he felt for his Dominant and now soon-to-be husband only felt overwhelming sometimes—like when they were in the midst of an intense scene or during aftercare, when both of them would often try to outdo the other with loving sentiments. But now, his love was fuller than he thought it ever could be. All he could think to do was hold Court's hand and pet the ring on his finger.

"Are you happy?" Court asked.

Lucan scoffed softly. "I'm like, drowning in happiness right now." And he was. He loved everything about his life these days: his job, his relationship, his circle of friends. He and Court had remained active in the kink scene, and though Dom had moved out of state (he and Lucan chatted online sometimes), Erin, Roland, Flame, and other new and old friends formed a wonderful support network for Lucan and Court. At first, when Lucan had started spending more time around her, Cally had been cold to him. But she'd since realized that Lucan was here to stay this time. And he was.

"I'm happy, too," said Court. He held Lucan's chin and looked into his eyes. "Can you believe we get to spend every day together now?"

"Uh, can you believe we're going to get *married*?"

Court laughed. "Barely. I wasn't sure you'd say yes."

Lucan shook his head. "Unbelievable." Then he hooked his arms around Court's sweat-damp neck and whispered into his ear, "Yes, yes, yes, yes, yes..."

ALSO BY LYSS EM

Escorting the Escort

Writing as Lyssa Dering

Series: Wish City

How to Love a Monster

How to Tame a God

Box Sets

Paranormal Novellas Box Set

Standalones

Fangs Like Me

Babyvamp

Breaking Hell's Rules

fangjunkie27

Lovesick

Belly Up

ABOUT THE AUTHOR

Lyss Em, who has been writing under the pen name **Lyssa Dering** since 2015, is the author of *How to Love a Monster*, *Babyvamp*, and several other indie-published titles, as well as *Fangs Like Me*, published with NineStar Press. Since her first foray into *Harry Potter* fanfiction, Lyss has been drawn to twisted, angst-filled M/M pairings. Under **Lyssa Dering**, she has so far written about a brain-eating antihero (*How to Love a Monster*), a high-tech matchmaking program gone wrong (*Lovesick*), and a brooding dhampir letting his savage side loose (*fangjunkie27*), with more fantastical ideas always lurking. Under **Lyss Em**, she writes contemporary erotic romance.

Lyss resides in the Midwestern United States with an aggressively affectionate tabby cat. When not writing, she fancies herself a connoisseur of "trash"—devouring the highest quality kinky, enemies-to-lovers, and dubious consent M/M she can get her hands on. Lyss is nonbinary and has no preferred pronouns—any are fine.

You can find Lyss primarily on Twitter, where she loves hearing from readers.

Connect with Lyss:
Website: lyss.press
Email: lyss@lyss.press

twitter.com/lysspress

facebook.com/lysspress

instagram.com/lysspress

goodreads.com/lyssem

bookbub.com/authors/lyss-em

pinterest.com/lyss_press

amazon.com/author/lyssem

www.ingramcontent.com/pod-product-compliance
Lightning Source LLC
Chambersburg PA
CBHW071113100726
47908CB00008B/2359